A HINT OF THIEF

A HINT OF THIEF (Justice #9)
ISBN-13 - 978-1-64918-032-2
Copyright 2023 by Suzan Harden
All rights reserved

Published by Angry Sheep Publishing
Findlay, Ohio

Cover Design by For the Muse Design
Interior Design by JW Manus

A Hint of Thief

Justice #9

SUZAN HARDEN

Bloodlines

Blood Magick
Zombie Love
Zombie Confidential
Zombie Wedding
Amish, Vamps & Thieves
Blood Sacrifice
Love, War & a Bulldog
Zombie Goddess
Ravaged
Sacrificed
Reality Bites
Ghouls in the Grocery
Resurrected
Bloodlines Shorts Anthology
Bloodlines: The First Boxed Set

Seasons of Magick

Spring
Summer
Autumn
Winter
The Seasons of Magick Anthology

Millersburg Magick Mysteries

Spells and Sleuths
Fae and Felonies
Magick and Murder

888-555-HERO

Hero De Facto
Hero Ad Hoc
Hero De Novo
A Very Hero Christmas
Hero De Jure
Hero In Camera
Hero Amicus Curiae
A Very Hero Wedding
A Very Hero New Year
Hero Ad Litem
Queer Eye for the Super Guy

Soccer Moms of the Apocalypse

Pestilence in Pumpkin Spice
Famine in French Vanilla
War in White Chocolate
Death in Double Mocha

Miscellaneous

Sword and Sorceress 31 ("Pig-Headed")
Sword and Sorceress 32 ("Unexpected")
Practical Witches
Revenge Served Hot
The Yule Switch
Chocolate for Dinner
Silver Shoes and Pigs' Ears

Crossover Worlds

Invasion!

Solar System Services, Inc.

Alone Is Not Lonely

For updates, news, and giveaways, join Suzan's mailing list or visit her website at www.suzanharden.com. You can also check her out on Facebook @SuzanHardenWriter.

Prologue

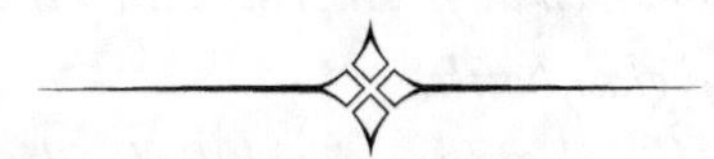

Love paraded around in the beautiful jewels and precious metals Conflict had gifted Her. However, Thief desired some of the lovely baubles for His own, and He asked His brother where He found such things.

"As Father taught Me, You must dig deep in the ground to find them, Little Brother," Conflict said. "I can show You the general areas where I found the different kinds of stones and ores."

"Stones and ores?" Thief exclaimed.

Conflict nodded. "But then You shape the stones and ores into the rings or bracelets or necklaces. Father can help You with the cutting and forging and molding as He did with Me."

"The jewels and the metals do not come out of the ground pre-formed?"

"Of course not!" Conflict guffawed. "Even Mother must pick Child's grain and grind it into flour in order to make Her cakes. Father must cut trees and chisel stone in order to make Our homes."

"That is an enormous amount of work!" Thief protested.

"Yes, it is," Conflict agreed. "But if You want some ornaments of Your own, then that is what You must do."

"Would You please make beautiful things for Me like You did Love?" Thief begged.

Conflict sighed. "With the work Balance has tasked Me, I no longer have the time to make such a quest. If You wish to trade Love for some of Her baubles, You should ask Her what She desires in exchange."

However, it made no sense to Thief why He should work so hard to obtain such pretty things when Love did not have to and She was still allowed to enjoy them, not Conflict. So, Thief devised a plan.

He carefully observed Love over the next several days. She only removed Her accessories while She bathed. He then procured sweet-smelling herbs from Child, added a few drops of soma tears from Vintner, and steeped everything in sweet oil for seven days. After straining the herbs, Thief poured the oil into a beautiful glass bottle.

He went to Love's home and presented the bottle of scented oil to Her. "A gift for You, My Sister."

"How thoughtful, Brother!" She smiled brightly. "What is the occasion?"

"I have been experimenting with products from Child's garden, attempting to create new items for trade." He bobbed His head. "With Your excellent taste, I want You to try this oil in Your bath. It will soften Your skin, and I believe You will appreciate the scent."

Love loosened the stopper and delicately sniffed the contents. "That is quite an intoxicating scent. If it lives up to your boasting as to its effects, I shall want more."

Thief suppressed His initial excitement. "Would You possibly consider trading another bottle of oil for that ruby You are wearing?"

She covered the jewel hanging around Her neck by a silver chain with Her hand. "I cannot give this to You. It was a gift from Conflict."

"Perhaps there is another jewel or bauble you might want to trade." Thief attempted to keep an innocent appearance.

"Oh, I cannot do that," She said. "The only ones I have are all gifts from Conflict. Perhaps I can write You a poem or a song. Or perhaps I can tell You a story."

"Oh, I have plenty of stories." He waved negligently. "If You change Your mind, please inform Me. In the meantime, I hope You enjoy Your gift."

Thief left Love's home. He had tried Conflict's suggestion, and it did not work. Then, He needed to do things His own way.

He waited and spied until Love poured the oil into Her bath. Once She was sound asleep from the soma tears, He entered Her dwelling and took the ruby and silver necklace along with a few other baubles.

Sometime later, a great clamor disturbed Thief as He admired the ruby in the sunlight. He hid the baubles before He raced in the direction of the uproar.

At Love's home, Mother and Child held Love Who wailed inconsolably. Father shouted at Conflict Who shouted right back. Wildling prowled around the dwelling in the form of a wolf and sniffed the grass. Balance, Light, and Death spoke quietly among themselves.

"What happened?" Thief asked.

Vintner and Knowledge exited the dwelling. "Someone slipped soma tears in Love's bath oil," Vintner said grimly. "While She slept, someone took Her favorite necklace."

"Who could have done such a thing?" Thief asked.

"There are only the Twelve of Us here," Knowledge said.

"Maybe Someone wanted His gifts back." Father glared at Conflict.

Wildling raised His head. "The most recent scents I detect are Love's and Thief's."

"I visited Love earlier to give Her a gift of the bath oil." Thief's mind spun, trying to find a way out of discovery of His deed. "But why would I take Her necklace? Conflict told Me how to find the materials to make adornments like the ones He made for Love."

Love ceased weeping, and Her swollen eyes narrowed. "You asked to trade more bath oils for My ruby."

"Really?" Knowledge scowled at Thief.

"Tell Us the truth, Thief," Light said. "Did You take Love's necklace?"
Thief bowed His head. "Yes."

Death sighed. "Why would You do such a thing?"

"They were very pretty, and I wanted them," Thief murmured.

Balance approached Him, and Her unseeing eyes pierced His very being. "We cannot violate One Another's sanctity. We do not steal from One Another."

Thief trembled. What if Balance banished Him as She once did with Conflict?

"Am I to be punished?" He murmured.

"No, but You will make restitution to Love by returning Her rocks and metals," Balance stated. "And then, You will use the knowledge Conflict shared with You to make a gift for the rest of Us."

Relief flooded Thief that He would not be banished. "I will give the baubles back to Love." He turned and trudged toward His lair.

But as He walked, envy seized His heart again. What if He ran away with Love's trinkets? Or what if He claimed they were stolen from Him and set the Others upon Themselves?

At the sound of footsteps behind Him, He whirled to find Father. "Why are you following Me?"

"I wanted to ask You a question." Father paused, a disappointed look in His eyes. "Why didn't You come to Me for assistance in making Your Own ornaments instead of taking Your Sister's?"

Shame flooded Thief. It was not an emotion He'd experienced before now, and it made Him angry. "I was jealous. No one ever gave Me such gifts."

"Oh, My Boy." Father sadly shook His head. "Gifts are not a measure of one's regard for another."

"But they're pretty, and Love has them all, and it's not fair," Thief wailed.

"Balance makes things fair, but not on Your schedule," Father gently chided.

"But—"

"And part of that fairness is learning to help Yourself," Father continued. "Conflict gave You the information You needed to create Your own pretty baubles. Laziness only begets problems for Everyone in Our community."

Father's wisdom permeated Thief. "Once I return Conflict's gifts, would You help Me create new types of jewels for Balance and the Rest of Our Family?"

Father agreed, and once Thief returned Love's baubles, They set to work. When They finished, Thief set each tiny crystal on Balance's cloak. The giant stone was set about Her neck. They were such glorious gifts Balance shared them with the World at night.

– The Tenth Book of Thief, Verses I thru LVIII

Chapter 1

I breathed in the air of my home world through the wave of vertigo caused by the Grey Ladies' portal. The sweet scent of cherry blossoms and other spring flowers brought tears to my eyes. Not from the pollen or the fading dizziness, but from the release of my emotions. Deep down, I had feared I would never be able to return.

The Grey Ladies deposited me where I had left my world, at the edge of the royal gardens near the square in front of the Crimson Palace in the capital of the Kingdom of Ryukyu. However, I was still thousands of leagues from Issura. I prayed to the Twelve I wasn't alone in the island nation.

As usual, none of our deities bothered to answer me.

The lack of sound in the royal square of the Ryukyuan capital of Naha unnerved me. Blood still stained the pavers of the square, and the gates of the Crimson Palace itself were closed. How long had it been since I fell through the portal the skinwalker had opened to allow one of the demons to escape?

Or perhaps the skinwalker's real goal had been to summon reinforcements from the demon realm. Either way, neither the demon nor I ended up in the demons' home dimension. What had happened while I was gone? How long *had* I been gone?

Time ran differently in different universes. I needed to remember to relay that information to my fellow justices Elizabeth, Yanaba, and Erato back at the Temple of Balance in Orrin. That was assuming I had access to Lady Shi Hua or another distance speaker. And that was assuming I'd arrived within a few hours of my unfortunate departure as the Grey Ladies had promised.

I took another deep breath, mainly to calm myself, and looked up at the sky. It was blank, a plain dark blue. No clouds impeded my vision. Definitely no bloody orbs floating above me. I released the air in my lungs. It was night. The next question was which night.

The best course of action would be to go back to the harbor. Surely, Captain Titus wouldn't have left Ryukyu without me. Luc wouldn't have let the *Mars Tranquilus* leave if I weren't onboard.

Except once again, I assumed both my love and the captain were still alive.

I considered calling out in silent speech, but I could end up attracting demons if the Ryukyuan Temples didn't vanquish the demon army that had attacked us in the square. I examined the walls of the Crimson Palace once again. No sentries. No lights.

Had Naha become like the handful of island villages of the western Peaceful Sea? The citizens had disappeared without a trace, taken by either skinwalkers or demons.

Or maybe something worse.

My best chance was to return to the harbor where the *Mars Tranquilus* had been berthed. I started walking down the main boulevard. The Ryukyuan Government House was actually divided into six different one-story buildings, three on each side of the street. There was no evidence of any humans, but of course, the bureaucratic offices would be closed after First Evening regardless of any demon attack.

The Ryukyuan government district bled into their Temple District, which again was oddly quiet. Night was the high time for worship at the Temple of Love. The paper sculptures the Ryukyuans used to light their streets were gone from their poles in this part of the city.

However, the wardens guarding the entrances to Vintner and Death raised the alarm the moment they spotted me walking down the thoroughfare. I stood still and clenched my fists to keep myself from reaching for my sword or knives as they converged on me. Unfortunately, my skill with the Ryukyuan language was far worse than my skill with Jing, so I remained silent at the shouted questions I couldn't comprehend.

As much as I wanted to resist the wardens' manhandling, I allowed myself to be shackled. Someone yanked back my hood, and a torch was thrust near my face. Squinting against the obscene brightness was totally involuntary on my part. A warden wrapped their arm around my throat, and another warden roughly forced my right eye open.

The wardens muttered amongst themselves, and then they reported their findings to the clergy who poured out of the nearby Temples. I blinked away the yellow afterimages of the damn torch. However, the yelling in the Ryukyuan language stopped.

"What day is it?" I asked in the Peaceful Sea trade tongue.

"You are breaking the island-wide curfew. Identify yourself," one of the Death priests demanded.

"I am Chief Justice Anthea DiBalance of Orrin from the Queendom of Issura. Which your wardens confirmed by poking me in the eye to make sure it was red," I added dryly.

Instead of introducing himself as etiquette demanded, he glared at me. "The Issuran chief justice fell into a demon summoning portal yesterday evening. For all I know, you are a demon wearing her skin."

The Temple bells started tolling. Not a demon alarm, but the time. First Night. If the Death priest spoke truly, I'd been gone for a little over a day in my world's time.

Despite the urge to argue with a priest simply performing his duties,

I took another calming breath. "Before you toss me into whatever gaol cell you plan to use, would you please send a message to the *Mars Tranquilus* to let my associates know I'm alive?"

The Death priest barked an order in Ryukyuan, and two of his wardens took off in the direction of Naha's harbor. "I am High Brother Gajoko. We will escort you to the Temple of Balance for additional questioning."

"That is satisfactory, High Brother." I couldn't bow with the chokehold around my neck. I hoped the priest didn't take offense to my failure to be polite. I'd encountered such illogical behavior before in Issura.

The forearm across my throat was removed, the wardens divested me of most of my weapons, and I shuffled from the weight of the shackles on my wrists and ankles down the street in the grip of two wardens. I merely hoped my friends were still alive and would arrive at the Temple of Balance before the Ryukyuan Reverend Mother decided it was better to behead me rather than take the chance I was under demon influence.

Chapter 2

Instead of being dragged to a gaol cell as I half-expected, High Brother Gajoko bade his wardens to guide me to a bench in the Temple of Balance's main courtroom. I sat with a contingent of wardens and clergy watching me while the Balance staff scurried off to wake whomever they needed to.

To my surprise, Chief Justice Fumiko entered the room on the arm of the Temple's chief warden a few moments later. I stood out of respect, which caused the warden to shove me back down to the bench.

"You do have a reputation for causing a commotion, Chief Justice Anthea," she said in Issuran.

"Surely, I would have thought my terrible reputation had circled the world a number of times before now, Chief Justice Fumiko. Forgive me for not greeting you as an equal, but your wardens seem terribly concerned for your safety."

"Like your wardens would not have done the same if our positions were reversed?"

We both laughed. Switching to the Peaceful Sea trade tongue, she bade the wardens to remove my shackles, much to High Brother Gojoko's consternation.

"Thank you," I said while I rubbed my wrists.

"Come with me, Chief Justice," she said. "Reverend Mother Yoshiko wishes to meet you while we wait for your compatriots."

"You mean she doesn't want a diplomatic incident with Issura."

She laughed again. "Nor with the Jing Empire. I fear the Crown Prince and his lady wife were as distraught by your disappearance as your own people."

I had brought Wardens Jonata and Long Feather from my own Temple of Balance in Orrin on this expedition because I trusted them to keep their heads in any occasion whether it be diplomatic or a battle. Which meant Luc had raised a terrible fuss when I disappeared through the portal.

"My acquaintance with Crown Prince Po began years ago when he was merely the Jing ambassador to Issura." I shrugged. "I did not know of his regard for me until he asked Queen Teodora to allow me to accompany him to Jing for his coronation as the official Issuran representative. I sincerely apologize for any problems he or High Brother Luc may have caused in my absence."

Chief Justice Fumiko bade High Brother Gojoko to return my blades to me. He reluctantly did so. His suspicions grated against my psyche, but no emotion showed on his visage.

As I sheathed my weapons once again, one of the Balance wardens stepped forward and bowed to me. "I am Warden Miyagi. It would be my privilege to act as your escort until your own wardens arrive, Chief Justice."

My impulsiveness had already cause a bit of a diplomatic mess. I couldn't chide the man for performing a traditional duty. Every other priestess of Balance, from the youngest novice to the Reverend Mother, depended on the wardens to act as their eyes. I was the only justice who could see.

After a fashion, that was.

"Your offer of service honors me." I held out my left hand. He gently grasped my fingers and wrapped them around his elbow. I stood, and this time, the Death and Vintner wardens didn't restrain me.

We followed Chief Justice Fumiko and her chief warden through the stone hallways of the first story of the Temple. Unlike the granite and marble used in Issura, they constructed their first floors with limestone. The upper floors were made of wood and paper. It sounded ridiculous at first until Sister Jasmine of Thief explained the prevalence of typhoons and ground quakes in in the Ryukuan islands.

The Ryukyuans also relied on Knowledge magic to light their buildings and streets. Given the construction materials and the nature of the islands, using such lamps reduced the incidence of fire when a fierce storm or a quake occurred as the lightweight materials prevented severe injury if they collapsed.

Not that I needed conventional light any more than I needed a warden to guide me. Well, that wasn't totally true. The fogs along the western Issuran coast inhibited my sight as much as they did conventional human sight.

Two wardens stood guard in front of the door at the end of the last hallway. As in my own Temple, no signs marked any of the doorways to the private quarters. I had kept count of the steps and turns in case I was forced to escape. I prayed I didn't need to do so.

On one side of Balance's scales, I hadn't spotted a demon or a skinwalker. But even my peculiar sight couldn't penetrate the spells that allowed a demon to wear a human skin. I could be surrounded and not even know it.

One of the wardens on duty opened the doors to the Reverend Mother's chambers and announced our presence. I think. He spoke in Ryukyuan so I couldn't be sure, though he definitely said my name.

We entered a sitting room that was modest, but the few furnishings and decorations were made of the finest quality. An elderly woman reclined on a chaise of mahogany and silk. Several pillows propped her to a sitting position, and blankets covered her legs. Her hood was pushed back, and her scalp held only a sparse selection of blue hairs. She had more strands on her wrinkled chin than the rest of her head.

I bowed along with Chief Justice Fumiko and the wardens who escorted us.

"Reverend Mother, the reports are accurate," Fumiko said. "The Issuran chief justice has returned to Naha."

Another's mind touched mine. Not intruding past my outer thoughts, just enough to see my talents.

The Reverend Mother chuckled and spoke in the trade tongue. "I am impressed you not only survived the demon realm, but they did not corrupt you."

For the first time, I truly believed High Sister Mya's analysis of my emotional and mental health. Orrin's seat of Child had spent two months caring for me after a demon grimoire impaled my psyche with its malevolent influence. I had been lucky Yanaba's squire Ming Wei's own empathic talents had ignited and saved my spirit.

"Forgive my correction, Reverend Mother, but I never reached the demons' realm despite their intentions," I said. "Brother Jin of Light killed the skinwalker who cast the portal spell. I believe a combination of his spell, the skinwalker's, and my time spell at the same moment to kill the demon I chased disrupted the portal."

The people in the room were totally silent for a very long moment.

"Where did you go, child?" the Reverend Mother finally asked.

"It's very complicated, Reverend Mother," I murmured. "May I beg your indulgence to wait until my associates have been notified of my whereabouts? It's late, and I would much like to only tell this tale once."

She said something to her aide, who bowed and exited the sitting room. "Shall we speak of more pleasant topics while we wait for our tea, Chief Justice?"

I inclined my head. "That would be more than acceptable, Reverend Mother."

She asked me questions about my travel outside of Orrin. I did my best to give her enjoyable descriptions, such as the sea wolves playing alongside our ship during our voyages, the stark and wild beauty of Diné, and the change of seasons during my circuits in the Gray Mountains.

The door opened, and the same warden who announced me only said a few words before the new guests rushed past him. I rose at the commotion and was immediately enveloped in hugs.

Luc. Jonata. Long Feather. Quan. Shi Hua. Even Reverend Father Biming, the head of Jing's Temple of Thief. They embraced me, all talking at the same time, both out loud and silently.

And swimming in their love was the happiest moment of my life.

Chapter 3

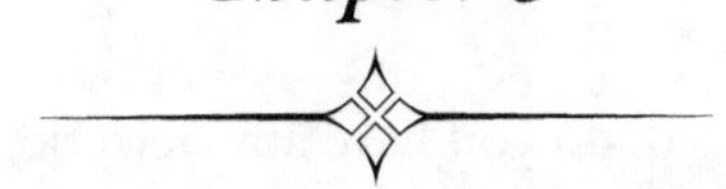

Despite never wanting this moment to end, I switched back to the trade tongue. "Please, everyone, we are being incredibly impolite to Reverend Mother Yoshiko. This is her Temple after all."

"It is quite all right, Chief Justice." A broad smile lit her wrinkled face. "We all need to enjoy good fortune when Thief grants it."

She ordered her staff to bring us more tea and some light fare, and she asked for one of her clerks to attend us. No one else ate more than a few bites, but I was extremely hungry. In between morsels, I told the tale of my strange adventures after I fell through the skinwalker's portal.

Everyone was astounded by some of the things I described. In fact, the clerk asked me to stop and repeat some statements because she was so entranced by my peculiar tale at times she forgot to take notes.

"I'm not sure if that's a total wagonload of horseshit, or if this really happened to you," Reverend Father Biming proclaimed when I was finished. Quan and Shi Hua stared at him for his audacity, even if I was lower ranked in the Temple hierarchy.

I shrugged. "One of you could truthspell me, and Reverend Mother Yoshiko or Chief Justice Fumiko could perform a formal interrogation."

Reverend Father Biming flushed a brilliant orange as he realized his insult.

"Really, Reverend Father?" Shi Hua clicked her tongue against the roof of her mouth three times. "You dare to call the Queen of Issura's ambassador a liar?"

"I beg your forgiveness, Lady Justice." Biming bowed his head. "My ill-chosen words are inexcusable."

"After the last three winters as a chief justice, I have neither the energy nor the desire to call you out, Reverend Father." I returned his bow. "All is forgiven."

"Now that is settled, do you have any objections to my clerks disseminating this information to the other nations' Reverend Mothers of Balance?" The Ryukyuan Reverend Mother appeared gravely concerned about my tale.

"I have no objections, Reverend Mother," I said. "However, I'd like the opportunity to review your clerk's transcript prior to it being sent out to clarify or add information I may have forgotten in my exhaustion."

"I think we could all use a good night's sleep after the excitement over the past two days." As she spoke, I noticed her coloring had faded from a medium yellow to a pale yellow. Fumiko had stated Reverend Mother Yoshiko wasn't well. Between the demon attack and being roused from her sleep at my return, we were wearing out the poor woman.

"May I be allowed to call on you after the midday meal, Reverend Mother?" I asked.

"We were—" Reverend Father Biming started, but with sharp glances from both Quan and Shi Hua, he cleared his throat and began again. "We would be honored to have you and Chief Justice Fumiko as our guests for the midday meal on board the *Unbridled*."

The Reverend Mother chuckled. "Ah, Thief Biming, you are as much as a scamp as your father was when we were novices."

The Reverend Father couldn't have looked more shocked if someone had tossed their cup of tea in his face. "Y-you knew my father?"

"It was a long, long time ago." Her wide smile showed some missing teeth. "I'm too old to be running around Naha. Come to Balance for the midday meal with Anthea. While she and Fumiko review her testimony, I can tell you some tales of your father."

Her expression turned sad. "We used to talk much more between our nations when I was younger. The failure to continue has hurt us all in the short term, which means we need to resurrect those older traditions. The Revelation of Balance says we still have twenty-one years of demon incursions to suffer through."

I glanced at Shi Hua, who nodded her agreement. After the last two years of working closely together, she knew my question without the need for silent speech.

"May Lady Shi Hua accompany the Reverend Father and me to your Temple tomorrow?" I requested. "As part of her instruction in diplomacy, of course."

Once again, the Reverend Mother laughed. "To make sure a Light accompanies you, or so Biming has eyes and ears everywhere?"

"Actually, I have found the lady's counsel to be a great asset in my own duties, Reverend Mother." I chuckled. "And between her and my wardens, I shouldn't fall into any more holes."

Everyone in the room, including the Ryukyuan wardens, deemed my comment highly amusing.

"As long as her husband has no objections," the Reverend Mother said. "I would not wish to start a diplomatic incident with the new ruler of a regional neighbor."

"As Chief Justice Anthea pointed out, I trust my wife to keep her out of trouble," Quan replied. "Given the recent demon attacks in both Jing and Ryukyu, we need to support and defend each other."

Amazement filled me. Whatever worries I had about Quan ascending to the Jing throne disappeared with his answer to the Reverend

Mother. And it reminded me Shi Hua was not Temple anymore. I could no longer rely on her assistance in certain matters. Or for much longer.

"Thank you, Your Highness, for this small kindness." I inclined my head to him. "I apologize for my presumption regarding your lady wife."

"No insult was taken, Chief Justice." His smile was gracious. "The two of you have become great friends, and I owe you her life. I would not presume to interfere in your relationship in the short time you have left."

"Not to interrupt your mutual admiration society, but it is late, and this old woman needs her sleep," the Reverend Mother said. "Until our visit tomorrow, my friends, may the Twelve bless your paths."

The Issuran and Jing contingents hastily rose at the Reverend Mother's dismissal. I offered a quick thanks to her before Chief Justice Fumiko and their Balance wardens escorted us from her presence.

How much longer? I asked Fumiko silently as the Balance escort walked us to the Naha docks.

Every day she remains with us is a blessing from the Twelve. The Ryukyuan justice's unease permeated our private link. *If she lives through the Spring Rituals, our Master Healer will be shocked.*

You will make a fine Reverend Mother when the time comes, I assured her.

Fumiko's self-deprecating laugh felt like glass beads clinking together. *She says the same thing, but I fear I will not live up to her excellence.*

No, you will have to do better. I sent a thread of empathy for her position. *Yesterday's demon incursion is the first one in Ryukyu during her tenure, isn't it?*

Yes.

And you led the Balance forces in the battle against the demons?

Yes.

Naha and the Kingdom of Ryukyu still exist to fight another day. I would call your first combat experience a rousing success, and you will do just fine leading your Temple as a whole.

Fumiko laughed her glass-bead laugh. *I can see why the Jing crown prince trusts you. Such logic can uplift while being practical.*

The real practicality facing me was completing my mission and seeing Quan take the Jing throne without enduring anymore losses. And I still didn't know the fate of all who fought in front of the gates of the Crimson Palace what was for me several days ago.

Chapter 4

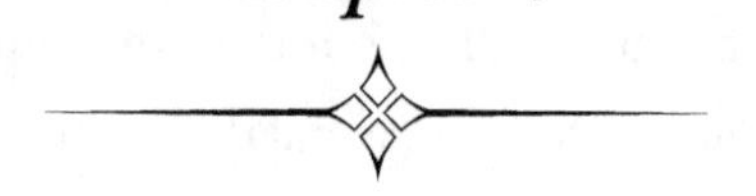

Reverend Father Biming parted from us to clamber aboard the *Unbridled*. To my surprise, Quan and Shi Hua followed Luc, my wardens, and me onboard the *Mars Tranquilus*.

Completely out of character and violating a number of etiquette rules, the captain, officers, and crew of the Issuran ship embraced me before I could take more than two steps onto the main deck. Several of them requested my tale of how I survived the demon realm before Captain Titus proclaimed it was late, and I needed rest. I promised to regale the crew with my story once we settled matters in Naha and continued on to Jing.

Jonata guided me to our cabin. The interior was crammed with the rest of the ship's passengers, including little Yin Shang. The child threw his pudgy arms about my waist and clung to me like a leech. Most of what he said was in Jing and mangled by his sobs. His fear and relief mirrored my own emotions, and I found myself weeping while I hugged the members of our party who could not go to the Temple of Balance.

Mateqai was alive, but nasty scars marred his handsome face and his right forearm. Balance only knew how bad his injuries were under his clothing.

"I feared we lost you when you were separated from Shi Hua during the battle," I said.

"I shared the same fear." His smile was crooked with the scarring, but the expression held the same warmth. "I was knocked unconscious by the flashbang that killed the demon attacking me. I awoke beneath a pile of bodies, both human and demon. Thankfully, the Ryukyuan Temple of Death were efficient and found me when I started shouting, but not so efficient I was laid on the funeral pyres before I regained my senses."

Jonata led me to the bed I shared with Luc during our voyage. Luc sat beside me and laid his crutches in the bottom storage drawer under the bed. He clasped my right hand in his left so tightly I feared our flesh would meld together, but I welcomed the pain.

Yin Shang climbed upon the bed on my left. His mother Sister Yin Li of Love was about to chide him, but I caught her attention and shook my head. She pursed her lips and relented. We were all too emotional to start any arguments at the moment, even over something like a mother attempting to instill etiquette and manners in her offspring.

I told my companions who hadn't been at the Temple of Balance an abbreviated version of my misadventures and how I returned to Naha. I said I would tell the remainder in the morning if they wished to join the officers and crew for our morning meal.

"Is there anything you left out during your recitation to the Reverend Mother?" Quan asked. In other words, had I withheld information for a reason from the Ryukyuan Temples?

"Nothing intentional," I assured him. "However, I am thoroughly exhausted. That's why I wanted to review the dispatch before she sends it to the other Temples of Balance on the morrow."

I narrowed my eyes. "My question is why aren't you, Lady Shi Hua, and the rest of your party taking up quarters on the *Unbridled*. That was the plan so you would arrive in Jing in a style befitting an emperor."

It was nothing personal against the *Mars Tranquilus*. However, its design was over a generation old. The brand new carrack design of the *Unbridled* was half again the size of the caravels comprising most of Issura's trading fleets. I understood Biming's desire to move Quan and Shi Hua to the grander ship. Jing was no different than Issura. Appearances were everything among the noble class.

"Because the safest place to keep my prince alive is by your side," Shi Hua said with a wicked grin.

"You didn't know if I would come back," I said sternly.

Everyone remained silent for a long time. I picked up anger and embarrassment from all of them.

Surprisingly, it was Warden Yar who broke the silence. "Captain Titus refused to leave without you, m'lady. Reverend Father Biming tried to convince the crown prince and his party to board the *Unbridled* and head for Jing. As Lady Shi Hua pointed out at the time, such an argument should not have taken place in front of the citizens of Ryukyu."

For the gentle giant to explain, there had been more than a simple difference of opinion between the Reverend Father of Thief and the soon-to-be emperor of Jing. The pair may have been lovers before Balance had separated them into their more profound roles in life, but I was fairly certain Biming's attitude had more to do with his fear that Quan's enemies would have more time to plan Quan's demise than any jealousy over Quan's marriage to Shi Hua. The fact the two self-assured and circumspect men lost their tempers in public was even more astounding.

I eyed Quan. "Should I assume the Reverend Father wished to sail with the first high tide on the morrow?"

"Actually, he wanted to leave on this evening's high tide. There is no reason we cannot stay an extra day for you to consult with the Ryukyuan Reverend Mother of Balance," he said dryly. "If demons are invading other worlds, not just our own, shared knowledge becomes an imperative. And the crew of the *Mars Tranquilus* can use the extra rest after our battle-laden voyage across the Peaceful Sea."

"Thank you for allowing your common sense and compassion to rule your decisions, Your Highness." I inclined my head.

"Let us hope my fellow citizens feel the same way you do, m'lady," he replied.

Shi Hua patted his arm. "Po, we all need some rest. Dawn will be here all too soon."

As if to confirm her evaluation, the Temple bells rang Third Night. I yawned.

"We'll discuss things in the morning," Luc promised Quan.

Once the Jing contingent of our expedition returned to their cabin, it was all I could do to remove my gear and clothing. Thankfully, no one treated me as an invalid. Instead Luc and the wardens made their own preparations for sleep. I yanked on my sleep shift and crawled onto the bed.

"Shi Hua's trousseau wouldn't be ready until midday tomorrow." I yawned. "Was Reverend Father Biming planning to leave without it?"

"I don't think her dresses were on top of his priority list at the time, m'love." Luc extinguished his spells on the alabaster globes that provided conventional light for the rest of my cabin mates.

I curled in the crook of his shoulder. *You haven't said much since I returned.*

I haven't had much of an opportunity. He kissed my temple. *I feared I'd never see you again when you ran straight into that rip in reality. I was terrified you had suffered a terrible fate in the demon realm. I didn't share Shi Hua's faith you would find a way home. I hope you can forgive me.*

I feared the same things you did, I said. *You've had so many terrible losses over the last two years. I can understand your despair, and I am so sorry I caused you to feel that way.*

He hugged me tightly. *I'm simply glad you are back with us. I love you.*

I love you, too.

Beneath my ear, his heartbeat slowed and his breathing deepened. However, sleep eluded me despite the fatigue dragging my limbs and mind.

We couldn't afford Quan and Biming fighting, whether it be in public or in private. We already knew the Jing nobility had never been happy with the idea of an emperor with Thief talent, much less one who had a common-born parent. Quan needed the support of the Temples and Guilds, but I wouldn't put it past the renegades to recruit some nobles to their cause.

If only the idiots knew they would be killed and eaten by the renegades' true allies once they murdered Quan.

Chapter 5

Knocking on our cabin door woke the five of us who were sleeping. Long Feather rose from the table where he had been writing in a small book. I reached out with my senses before he answered the door. Captain Titus stood outside. Long Feather stepped out on the deck. Male voices hummed, and Long Feather stepped back inside.

Luc sat upright next to me. "We're all awake. What does the captain need?"

"Sisters Jade and Jasmine have arrived with a message. Lady Shi Hua's trousseau is ready, and since the chief justice paid for everything, she needs to inspect the dresses and sign for them."

I groaned. "What is the hour, Warden?"

"Approximately a half candlemark past Second Morning, m'lady."

"Three periods of sleep is better than nothing." I rubbed my eyes. "Has he informed Lady Shi Hua yet?"

"I don't know, m'lady."

I concentrated. *Shi Hua?*

I'm on the pier. Sisters Jade and Jasmine are here. They said they are delivering a message from the dressmaker to you—

Captain Titus delivered their message. Give me and the wardens a chance to dress and we'll meet you on the pier.

Shi Hua's laughter tinkled like the silver bells on a Love priestess's veil. *I will tell Reverend Father Biming to meet us at the Temple of Balance a few moments before First Afternoon.*

She definitely gave the impression she wanted to speak with Biming privately as she withdrew from my thoughts. Things had definitely changed between them. She was no longer the bodyguard of the third in line to Jing's Dragon Throne or a sister of Light. I doubted Biming expected his prized pupil to outrank him at such a tender age. The former sister would soon be the Empress Consort.

The first and most prominent spouse.

A title Quan's mother hadn't granted to her one legitimate husband.

It made me wonder if that was the real reason her husband joined the renegades. Had he or his family hoped to take over Jing through his marriage? Such a desire made the nobles' resentment of Quan as the eldest child logical.

Jonata and I quickly dressed while Long Feather fetched Mateqai. Long Feather had been acting as Yin Li's warden for the duration of our voyage as Mateqai had been acting as Shi Hua's. Even though she had been granted dispensation to leave Light in order to marry Quan, Mateqai had stayed by her side. He almost seemed relieved he was coming with me to the market district of Naha instead of remaining onboard the *Mars Tranquilus*.

In addition, Captain Titus assigned two of his sailors to accompany us. "Just in case," he said. I'd become well acquainted with Sea Wolf and Little Squirrel during the course of our voyage across the Peaceful Sea, and I welcomed their presence on our jaunt across the city.

There was a definite sense of unease in the air as we walked down the gangplank. Jade and Jasmine's muscles tensed beneath their exposed skin, the rush of blood through their vessels obvious to my queer sight. Even my non-talented wardens and sailors shot furtive glances left and right in their attempts to suss out a potential threat.

The two Ryukyuan Thief priestesses brought their own wardens with them this time, though the sisters dressed as wealthy merchants and the wardens as their mercenary guards.

"I hear everyone in the city is concerned about another demon attack," I said, foregoing any formal greeting.

"There is also much concern over your return from the demon realm," Jade spat.

"What do you wish to know?" I said as evenly as possible.

Jade stepped closer to me, an ugly expression on her face and her hand on what appeared to be a ceremonial knife. I doubted the knife was merely decorative. I also doubted it was the only weapon on hers and Jasmine's persons.

"How did you survive? No human who has entered one of their portals has ever come back."

"I survived because I never made to the demon domain." After all my fear and anxiety I would never make it back to my home world, to have everyone question my integrity was irritating. But I would act with similar suspicion for the same reason if a different priestess returned with the same bizarre story. "Somehow, my magic interacted with the demon magic. It resulted in us landing near Death's domain. She took me and the other women trapped in the between place she called Otherwhere to Balance who returned me to Naha."

It would only make things more confusing if I tried to explain that the Grey Ladies were another aspect of Balance. They said they would have to place me a few hours after I left so I wouldn't step into the middle of the battle in front of the Crimson Palace. They wanted me alive. I still didn't understand why, nor did they care to inform me of their reasoning.

I prayed my new friends were also back at their homes. Both women had spouses and children they'd left behind. While I technically had neither, I would have been devastated never to see Luc or my squire Nathan again.

"You may have convinced the Reverend Mother of Balance of your innocence," Jade hissed. "But Thief is not so easily fooled."

I glanced at Sister Jasmine. Her expression was as placid as a cow's. So, her partner initiated the personal attack while she watched for weaknesses. Fine. I could play such games, too.

"Obviously, the Ryukyuan Temple of Thief can be fooled," I said dryly. "Or were you instructed to keep me occupied with Lady Shi Hua's trousseau so I didn't accidentally see the skinwalkers prior to the attack at the Crimson Palace?"

Sister Jasmine suddenly appeared nervous. "Are you accusing our Temple of assisting the renegades?"

"No, I'm accusing members of your Temple of being renegades." I sighed with an exaggerated air. "Your clergy wouldn't be the first to be seduced by their promise of power, but I also know what happens to their allies. My birth mother, who was a High Sister of Love in Issura, turned herself into a skinwalker in her quest for power."

At my words, Sister Jade stopped her verbal attack. "What?"

"My birth mother has been trying to kill me since I was in her womb." I stepped closer to Jade. "I excel in survival. I've been lucky to evade numerous plots to kill or convert me. And for whatever Their reasons, two of the Twelve want me alive and helping the Temples. And so far, that service has involved rooting out renegade sympathizers within the clergy."

"And given that I'm on the top of the renegades' list in the contract they have with the Assassins Guild, my guess is Light wants the chief justice to keep me alive." Shi Hua's baleful glare was enough for Jade to step back from me.

"We are here to serve, Lady Shi Hua, Chief Justice Anthea," Jasmine murmured with a bow. "We did not lie. The trousseau is ready."

"I, however, don't appreciate being tested in this manner," I snarled.

"We'll explain things at the dress shop, Chief Justice," Jasmine said in Issuran.

The Ryukyuan clergy were full of surprises.

I just hoped I could keep up without landing myself in yet another trap.

<h1 align="center">*Chapter 6*</h1>

The late morning walk to the dressmakers' shop was rather warm and pleasant, a reminder the Spring Rituals would start soon. However, the market and businesses were far quieter than my first trip through Naha's commercial district. A sensation of dread permeated the city.

The oddest part was the lack of children running through the streets. Two days ago local time, the markets were teeming with children playing or running errands for their parents.

Shi Hua, where are the children? I asked silently.

The little ones are in the Temples with enough mothers to watch and entertain them. The lady didn't look at me. *The older ones are at the Crimson Palace, assisting the civilian army with their preparations.*

From her slight sense of distraction and irritation, I withdrew and asked no further questions. Her emotions weren't aimed at me. Were the realities of her new role permeating her? Shi Hua had come a long way from being a farm girl. As part of the Temple of Light, she was expected to forgo intimate relations. Marrying the crown prince of her nation had to twist her emotions.

I had no doubt Quan would lean on her for her advice and sensible nature. Maybe there were other costs I failed to calculate when negotiating her marriage contract on her behalf?

We reached the dress shop, but the front door was closed. Jasmine knocked on the door instead of entering. Several clicks followed, locks being released, before the door opened, and the apparent chief of the shop waved us inside. Thick wool curtains covered every window. So, it wasn't just me who couldn't see into the main area of the storefront. The chief relocked the doors before she bowed to me and spoke in Ryukyuan.

Jade translated. "The trousseau is completed. However, Mistress Sachiko would like to make sure Lady Shi Hua's dresses fit as they should."

I nodded, and Mistress Sachiko and the two women with her all bowed to me and then to Shi Hua. The new bride followed them back toward the changing room. The women weren't happy about Warden Mateqai following them. But Jasmine pointed out he would be less likely to behead the seamstresses for making the wrong move in regards to Shi Hua than I would. And I had to agree with her. The ladies acquiesced to the warden's presence.

What I wasn't expecting was Reverend Father Ogusuku, the head of the Ryukyuan Temple of Thief, stepping out of the changing room. He smiled at me and bowed, an unusual measure since he outranked me.

He straightened and said in the Peaceful Sea trade tongue, "While the seamstresses finalize the Empress of Jing's wardrobe, we can discuss your odd adventure."

Shi Hua and Mateqai both paused and eyed me. I gave a slight shake of my head. I trusted mine and Jonata's skills if there was trouble with the Ryukyuan Thief clergy.

Like Sisters Jade and Jasmine, the Reverend Father dressed as a prosperous Ryukyuan merchant. Two wardens in mercenary garb accompanied him.

I couldn't help frowning at him, and I folded my arms over my chest. "Do you also believe I lied about what happened? I've already had

Reverend Father Biming call my testimony to your Reverend Mother of Balance a load of horseshit."

Surprisingly, he laughed at my crude wordage. "My Jing counterpart has too much resting on his shoulders at the moment. He might not be thinking straight. I doubt he meant to offer you insult, but the fact that he did worries me." He switched to heavily accented Issuran. "There is more riding on the success of your mission than you realize, Chief Justice. He feels my sister at Balance was not as thorough in her interrogation of you as she should have been."

I narrowed my eyes. "Do you wish to truthspell me?"

"Yes."

It was my turn to laugh. "And what makes you think you're a better interrogator than one of your justices?"

"No, I do not believe I am." He had the self-awareness to appear uncomfortable. "I hope you'll agree to be truthspelled when you go to the Temple of Balance."

"In other words, Biming doesn't want Quan to know what the two of you are up to," I snapped. "You do realize Lady Shi Hua is in the next room and can hear everything you say."

The lady in question charged out of the changing room, dressed in a lovely Jing dress and coat. "And I've already relayed your shenanigans to my husband."

Her hands heated from her talents, and for an instant, I feared she might incinerate Reverend Father Ogusuku.

"My lady, please allow the seamstresses to finish your final fitting," I murmured in the trade tongue. "I've paid good coin for your outfits."

I don't want to leave you alone with him, Anthea, she said silently.

And I wish to return to the Mars Tranquilus *before your husband does something stupid to the head of a Jing Temple,* I replied. *Not even I can save him if he harms Biming.*

"Reverend Father," I continued aloud in Issuran though I could feel Luc listening to my conversation through Shi Hua. "These very machinations are the reason the crown prince of Jing asked me and High Brother Luc to accompany him home. His father was hexed and is dying. His brother and nephews were assassinated. And now, Reverend Father Biming is plotting against him. How would you react if you were in Crown Prince Po's position?"

Reverend Father Ogusuku frowned before he nodded. "I do understand the crown prince's concerns. I am not saying this is the route I would take if I were Reverend Father Biming. As for my personal opinion, I also fear the effects of a Jing civil war on this part of the Old Continent. If such a conflict breaks out, it won't remain within Jing's borders. However, as the head of my Temple, I need some assurances you have not lied and haven't been corrupted by the demons because if you have been, the human race is doomed. What would you do if you were in my position?"

I couldn't fault Reverend Father Ogusuku's logic. "I do understand your worries, but if Reverend Father Biming was that concerned about truthspelling me, he should have been adamant with your Temple of Balance last night instead of insulting me."

"On that matter, we can both agree," Reverend Father Ogusuku said genially.

"Does the Reverend Mother know you are joining us for the midday meal at Balance?"

"She and Chief Justice Fumiko asked for my opinion of you." Reverend Father Ogusuku smiled. "And yes, they invited me."

"To head off any problems with Reverend Father Biming?" I smiled in return.

"It's best to keep the dissension between two separate nations to a minimum on our own shores." He bowed before he and his wardens entered a storeroom. From the vibrations in the floorboards, the seamstresses had a trapdoor to access to the Naha tunnel system.

The knowledge made me a little sad we had to destroy the entrances to Orrin's system after my birth mother compromised our security. A necessary move, though. I wondered how our High Brother Talbert of Thief handled the change, but I dare not ask. And after the horror the sisters of Love went through at my birth mother's hands, they rejoiced when the Miners Guild closed the tunnels.

Such idle musings occupied me while the seamstresses finished any final adjustments in Shi Hua's trousseau. The Ryukyuan women were a tad disappointed when Shi Hua refused to wear any of the outfits, but as she explained to the women, she couldn't afford to attract such attention to herself. Not without more guards.

Mateqai and Jade closely examined the trunk I had purchased along with the outfits. The warden and priestess seemed confident no deadly traps existed to catch the new empress unaware.

"Sea Wolf, could you take the trunk back to the *Mars Tranquilus* for us?" I asked politely.

The sailor nodded.

"Warden Jonata, would you please guard Sea Wolf on his trek to the docks?" I held up my hand when she opened her mouth to protest. "I trust Little Squirrel to watch my back as much as I trust you to ensure nothing will happen to Sea Wolf or Lady Shi Hua's belongings."

Jonata nodded curtly. "I will meet you at the Temple of Balance—"

"No, you will inform High Brother Luc of all my conversations with everyone from the Ryukyuan Temple of Thief." I glared at both Jade and Jasmine. "You will obey his instructions as you would my own until I return to the ship."

Jonata's displeasure at my orders grated along my psyche, but she crisply answered, "Yes, Chief Justice."

However, I feared once my warden and I were alone, I would definitely be getting an earful. And if anything did happen to me, she would take her wrath out on the two Thief priestesses.

Chapter 7

After Jonata and Sea Wolf left with the trunk, I added extra coins as a thank you to the seamstresses for finishing Shi Hua's trousseau on time despite a demon attack on Naha. The three women tried to graciously decline my gift, but Jade laughed and said something in their language.

Once again, I glared at the Thief priestess and demanded, "What did you tell them?"

"That it would be best not to anger a savage from the other side of the world because her tongue is sharper than her blades," Jade answered.

My mouth dropped open at her blatant insult. However, Jasmine and the three seamstresses tittered behind their hands. Even Shi Hua and Mateqai smirked. Little Squirrel did her best to imitate Jonata's worried and watchful attitude.

"Maybe my tongue wouldn't be so sharp if yours wasn't the whetstone," I snapped.

"Come, Chief Justice." Shi Hua stepped forward and linked her right arm with my left. "We have another appointment, and Captain Titus will be most vexed if he loses Little Squirrel because she defended your honor."

Shi Hua was correct. This wasn't a battle worth fighting. I managed to convey my gratitude to the dressmakers in the few words of

Ryukyuan I'd picked up since our arrival, and my effort seemed to be appreciated. Unfortunately, the priestess pricking my ego would be accompanying us to the Temple of Balance.

As we walked up the main boulevard, youths of all genders appeared on the street, rushing this way and that. However, all of them wore Temple staff uniforms. They were armed, and their miens were quite serious, carrying messages and performing tasks that would normally be carried out by the younger children.

Regret yanked at my swollen ego. One hundred years of relative quiet had made the human race complacent. Now, we were forcing our young into adult tasks long before they were ready. How did my great-grandparents deal with such issues when they were that age? They were the last generation to see combat with our invaders.

As we passed the Temple of Mother, I noticed a long line of civilians entering the outer courtyard of Balance. Silence reigned, and the surrounding Temples were abnormally quiet for the time of day despite the recent demon attack. Jasmine paused and spoke with a Balance warden, who kept part of his attention on the crowd. Her face fell and a single yellow tear trickled down her face.

I didn't need to speak to anyone or listen to their thoughts. A miasma of grief filled the Temple District. The Reverend Mother of Balance had passed.

Jasmine returned to our group. "Chief Justice Fumiko would still like to meet with you today, Chief Justice Anthea."

"I grieve with you." The formal words seemed inadequate for the occasion. I barely knew the woman, but she regarded my testimony as truth when none of her counterparts in the Kingdom of Ryukyu believed me.

The wardens had queues set up in the Temple's front garden. The civilians carefully hung paper butterflies from the trees or sat them on benches. As curious as I was about their mourning traditions, now wasn't the time to ask impertinent questions.

Two Balance wardens escorted my party past the civilians paying their respects, through the inner gate, and up the steps of the Temple itself. Chief Justice Fumiko and her chief warden waited for us beside the statue of Balance herself. And like the figure that stood in my own Temple in Orrin, She was carved from a single piece of basalt. Her stone hood covered her face and Her hands were clasped. However, this statue held a sword, though court was not in session.

Reverend Mother Yoshiko's own sword.

"We share your grief," I said as I bowed to Fumiko.

"For every life, there is a death." She sniffed delicately, trying to maintain her composure. "And we all see Light in the end."

"Surely, a junior justice can interrogate me regarding my statement from last night," I murmured. "I don't wish to intrude on any more of your duties or your mourning than I already have, m'lady."

"This is one duty I do not find onerous." She reached for my hand and clasped it as if she could see it. *You're not the only one with an unusual talent, Anthea. I can see a person's past when I touch them. I know about how the renegades tried to use your birth mother and a demon grimoire to corrupt you. I can't afford to give Thief anymore ammunition in their paranoia, I need to be present to control the path of your interrogation. Examine my soul to know I speak truly.*

I found it difficult to control my apprehension at Fumiko's confession regarding my secret. The Temple seats in Orrin closely guarded the truth, believing the renegades would use it to get me executed.

Who else knows besides your Reverend Mother?

No one, Fumiko answered fiercely. *You're not the only justice they've tried to seduce to their cause. I promise to explain everything once Reverend Father Ogusuku and Reverend Father Biming are satisfied.*

And if I can't satisfy them? I asked.

You're not the only one who may find their head parted from their shoulders by First Morning.

Chapter 8

For the first time, Shi Hua truly regretted parting from the Temple of Light. She didn't dare intrude on whatever Chief Justice Fumiko and Anthea were discussing silently, though she had a very strong suspicion it involved the odd visit from Reverend Father Ogusuku at the dress shop and Reverend Father Biming's paranoia concerning Anthea's disappearance and return. However, Shi Hua had become very fond of the chief justice of Orrin, and there were other ways she could help prevent the Balance priestess from losing her head.

High Brother Luc?

Yes, m'lady?

Even though her former superior addressed her properly, the change in their relative rank made her a tad uncomfortable.

We may have an issue here at the Temple of Balance, she said. *Has Warden Jonata returned to the* Mars Tranquilus *yet?*

Not yet. There was a long pause before Luc added, *Your husband would like to join our link.*

As much as she liked and respected Po, he could be rather bull-headed. Especially when it came to someone he was physically attracted to, like Anthea, but his attitude was something Shi Hua had dealt with for the last eight years. She prayed to Light she could manage it now.

Very well, she conceded. Once she felt Po's presence, she said, *Bao Quan Po, I'm treading a delicate line because this is a Temple matter—*

You are no longer Temple, he snapped.

Really? she said dryly. *I wasn't aware.*

Jonata and Sea Wolf have returned, Luc interjected.

"Lady Shi Hua?"

She jerked at Anthea's question, uncomfortably aware the Ryukyuan Balance chief warden, Little Squirrel, and the contingent from the Ryukyuan Temple of Thief were staring at her. "I'm sorry, Chief Justice."

"Are you all right?" Anthea eyed her with concern.

"I haven't slept well the last two nights." Shi Hua shrugged. "I beg your pardon. You were saying?"

"Would you be amenable to one of the Ryukyuan Light clergy performing the truthspell on me?" A sly smile spread across Anthea's face.

Shi Hua wanted to curse at herself. The chief justice must have figured out what she was really doing, but she wasn't objecting to Shi Hua consulting with High Brother Luc.

At this point anyway.

"As long as I am present during the truthspell and interrogation, I have no objection to another member of Light casting the actual spell." Shi Hua glared at the Thief contingent. "However, I do object to Thief's insinuations regarding your integrity. I want that on the record, Chief Justice Fumiko."

"Your objection to this whole circus will be added along with my own." Fumiko appeared as displeased as Shi Hua felt. "Reverend Father Ogusuku forgets I will be confirmed as the new Reverend Mother after my predecessor's funeral this evening. I have no problem calling a convocation shortly afterward."

The unspoken accusation Reverend Father Ogusuku was attempting to interfere with the succession of another Temple hung in the air.

Both Sisters Jade and Jasmine tried to protest that was not the case, but the surrounding staff and clergy of Balance didn't look convinced.

Lady Shi Hua, Warden Jonata has informed us of the situation with the Ryukyuan Temple of Thief, Luc murmured at the back of Shi Hua's mind. *Perhaps you and Anthea should politely decline the Reverend Mother of Balance's invitation.*

Unfortunately, that's the other problem, Shi Hua said. *We're already at the Temple of Balance. Reverend Mother Yoshiko passed away early this morning.*

Is there an issue with succession? Po asked.

Not within the Temple of Balance itself, she answered. *However, Reverend Father Ogusuku is trying to intimidate Chief Justice Fumiko prior to her formal installation later tonight. I fear he is using Reverend Father Biming for political gain within his own nation.*

And he's using Anthea falling through the damn demon gateway to do it, Luc growled. *Is Reverend Father Ogusuku blaming you or any of the Issurans for the Reverend Mother's death?*

Not yet. Shi Hua listened to a bit of Anthea and Fumiko's conversation before she returned to her own. *Thief is insisting on truthspelling Chief Justice Anthea. I made sure I will be present during the interrogation and someone from Light will perform the actual truthspell. Please, have Captain Titus prepare for a fast departure if we find it necessary.*

High tide? That only gives you a candlemark, Luc pointed out.

I am aware, High Brother, Shi Hua replied. *We may not have a choice about running for the ship.*

Do you want me to speak to Biming? Po's anger trickled through the link, though she could feel his effort to keep his temper under control.

No, Shi Hua and Luc said at the same time.

I will address his issues after I've dealt with this matter, Shi Hua added.

I'm his friend— Po started.

Which is exactly why I need to be the one to talk to him, my husband, Shi Hua said gently. *High Brother, if the captain has any issues, please let me know.*

She withdrew from the link to find Warden Mateqai standing almost inappropriately close to her. His right eyebrow rose. Of course, he suspected what she'd been doing, too.

"We need to leave as soon as possible so the *Mars Tranquilus* can make the afternoon tide," she whispered in Issuran.

Thankfully, he didn't question whose idea it was to leave earlier than planned. Light help her, she was going to miss him when he returned to Orrin.

The same Balance warden who escorted them into Balance entered with Reverend Father Biming and Reverend Father Ogusuku, their respective wardens, and the Ryukyuan Reverend Mother of Light with her wardens. The Balance chief warden whispered in Fumiko's ear, letting her know who had arrived. She pursed her lips, the only sign of her irritation.

Shi Hua couldn't blame her. With the Temples rigid hierarchy, Fumiko probably felt like the other seniors were throwing their weight around since she technically wasn't a Reverend Mother for a few more hours. Which in the case of Thief, that's exactly what they were doing.

Shi Hua reached out toward the docks once again. *Reverend Father Jin?*

Is there something wrong, my lady?

Please have our ships ready to depart with the afternoon high tide, Reverend Father. She tried to balance her sense of urgency with proper respect. *I've already asked High Brother Luc to do the same with the* Mars Tranquilus, *and I've informed the crown prince for the reason for the rapid departure.*

It will be done, but I request an explanation once we're underway, my lady.

Relief washed through her that Reverend Father Jin was taking the matter seriously. *Of course, Reverend Father.*

Two steps down. Now, she needed to get Anthea out of the Temple of Balance and down to the docks.

Preferably with the chief justice's head still attached to the rest of her.

Chapter 9

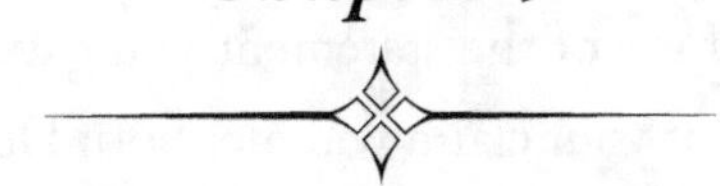

Shi Hua was up to something. Of that, I was sure. I felt her speak with Luc a moment ago. Now she silently spoke with another Light priest. With Warden Mateqai's serious demeanor, I hoped it involved getting me out of this awkward situation.

The Ryukyuan Reverend Mother of Light was probably my fellow justice Elizabeth's age. She hadn't bothered to wear her hood. Her hair was braided and pinned up with gold sticks similar to the silver ones worn by the Ryukyuan wardens. She carried an air of annoyance, whether because she had been dragged from her own Temple over a minor matter or she found Reverend Father Ogusuku's arrogance as detestable as Fumiko did.

"Reverend Mother Asako, this is Chief Justice Anthea of Issura," Fumiko said in the trade tongue.

Ignoring the two Thief Reverend Fathers, I bowed to the Reverend Mother of Light. "Greetings, Reverend Mother," I said in my best Ryukyuan.

Unfortunately, the Reverend Mother rattled a response so fast I couldn't understand a word. I held up my hand and switched to the trade tongue. "My apologies, Reverend Mother. You just heard half of my Ryukyuan vocabulary."

She chuckled. "My own apologies for making the assumption you knew our language, Chief Justice. Your pronunciation was impeccable. Shall we get your review of your statement done and over before the two Thief hens here lose all their feathers the way they are flapping about your survival?"

Both of the Reverend Fathers appeared taken aback, but Reverend Mother Asako didn't have any regard for their egos. "Reverend Mother Fumiko has apprised me of the statement you gave her predecessor. I am most curious about your claim you met both Death and Balance."

Her tone was conversational, not accusatory.

"I appreciate your assistance in putting any worries to rest before we continue our journey." I looked at Shi Hua. "The Jing emperor and his new bride are anxious to return home." I turned to Biming. "As I'm sure their Reverend Father of Thief is since he tried to leave Naha without me."

Biming's skin glowed a deep reddish orange. I wasn't sure if he truly believed I was a danger to Quan or if he was allowing Reverend Father Ogusuku to manipulate him. But whatever regard I felt for Biming was gone at this game he played.

I regarded Reverend Mother Asako once again. "As for my claim, I am sure the Reverend Mother of Balance will give you a copy of my testimony, so you may judge for yourself."

"Let us get this matter finished so the Jing emperor and his bride may be on their way," Reverend Mother Asako said. "Where would you like to do this, Reverend Mother Fumiko?"

"She is not the Reverend Mother of Balance yet," Reverend Father Ogusuku snapped.

"*Pfft.*" Reverend Mother Asako cocked her head. "Do you really want me to call a convocation over a few hours? And why are you dragging a foreign innocent into your games? A foreign innocent the Jing emperor holds in high regard?" She shifted as if she produced a throwing knife from beneath her sleeve. "Or are you a renegade hoping to finish off the Bao imperial line of Jing?"

"Are you calling me out?" Reverend Father Ogusuku's tone became frigid.

"Considering I'm number two on the Assassins Guild's list of targets, I am also wondering what your endgame is?" I kept my hands loose at my sides. The last thing we needed was a fight in the middle of the Ryukyuan Temple of Balance. How in the Twelve was I going to get Shi Hua out of here with only Mateqai and Little Squirrel as my rear guard?

As if in answer to my internal thought, the trio moved closer to me.

Warden Mateqai, I said silently. *If a fight breaks out, you and Little Squirrel are to do whatever it takes to get Lady Shi Hua back to the* Mars Tranquilus.

Before he could answer me, Balance wardens and justices rushed into the main courtroom. The majority quickly surrounded the Thief contingent. The remainder surrounded me, Shi Hua, and our escort, but it was a protective detail. Their attention was on the Thief clergy and wardens.

The same Balance clerk who had taken my statement last night set up her paper and inks on her desk by the dais of Balance's statue. "I am ready, Reverend Mother Fumiko."

"Chief Justice Anthea, do you mind if I make this truthspell?" Reverend Mother Asako asked.

"No, Reverend Mother," I answered.

She muttered her spell and made a quick gesture. The tingle of Light magic flowed across my skin.

Fumiko performed the typical opening questions of a formal interrogation to establish my name, origin, and rank. Then she surprised me by asking, "Did you intentionally lie at any point to my predecessor Reverend Mother Yoshiko last night?"

"No."

"Did you intentionally lie to me at any point last night?"

"No," I repeated.

"Thank you for your patience, Chief Justice Anthea." Fumiko smiled in my general direction. "Reverend Mother Asako?"

The Light magic melted away from my body.

"Chief Justice Anthea, a squad of my wardens and a squad of Light wardens will escort you and your parties back to your ships," Reverend Mother Fumiko said. "Will that be sufficient?"

"More than sufficient, Reverend Mother." I bowed to her. "I am merely sorry we lost the opportunity to converse socially again."

"We seem doomed never to have the opportunity." Her amusement faded. "Reverend Father Biming, my predecessor had some affection for your father. That is the only reason you are not sitting in a gaol cell for attempting to undermine my authority in my own Temple. You are hereby banished from the Kingdom of Ryukyu and any and all of her possessions for the period of five years. Is that understood?"

"Yes, Reverend Mother." His skin shone red with embarrassment. "I understand and will comply."

"May the Twelve guard your voyage to Jing, Lady Shi Hua," Reverend Mother Asako added.

"Thank you." Shi Hua bowed to the Reverend Mother of Light.

The Issuran Temple of Light needed to make some changes. By restricting its clergy to males, we were not using our queendom's full resources. And I had to trust that Fumiko and Asako would come to the truth of what their Reverend Father of Thief hoped to gain by accusing me of corruption.

Unless Shi Hua was right, and this was part of the renegades' plan to destroy the last of the Jing imperial family.

The squad of Balance wardens escorted us from the Temple. Across the boulevard, a squad of Light wardens waited. They fell in step around us once we were clear of the civilian mourners.

I had no doubt we would reach the docks safely and in time to depart with this afternoon's high tide. But I wondered if the Jing imperial family and the Jing Temples would survive today's split between them.

Chapter 10

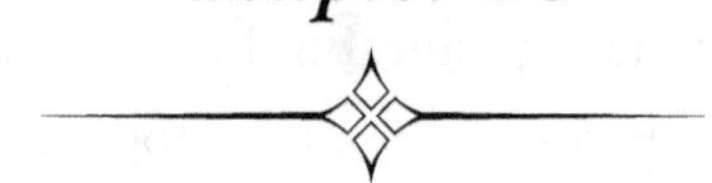

Shi Hua still seethed as the Ryukyuan wardens escorted the Issuran and Jing parties through the Naha market. Nothing had gone right on this damned trip. And to be betrayed by one of the few people she trusted demonstrated how difficult her new position in life would be.

"Lady Shi Hua—" Reverend Father Biming whispered in their own language.

She held up her hand. "Do not. Do. Not."

"You must understand—" he tried again.

"You and I will speak privately on board the *Unbridled*," she snapped. "And only then."

He nodded curtly, but the muscles along his jaw clenched and twitched.

Whatever faith she had in him over the years had been totally destroyed in a matter of days. And it would have to be addressed. Thank the Twelve, she'd been trained in most of Thief's tricks in preparation to be Po's bodyguard.

Po, are you and your guards on board the Unbridled? she asked silently.

Yes, dearest. Luc made arrangements for Warden Mateqai to join us. Is Biming giving you trouble?

Not more than he gave Anthea. The masts of the ships poked over the scarlet tile roofs of the low-slung warehouses surrounding the harbor. *However, I need to address some matters with Reverend Father Biming.*

May I ask the problem?

The emperor's concubine needs to understand that his attempt to manipulate a rival's death will not be tolerated.

Shi Hua noticed Mateqai didn't question her boarding the *Unbridled*, despite the events at the Temple of Balance. He simply followed her up the gangplank. Technically, she couldn't order him to join her, but she was thankful Luc had issued the order to his warden. She needed at least one person she could trust on board the Jing carrack.

She waited for Biming to issue the orders to depart. Now, that Po was onboard the *Unbridled*, the other three captains arranged their own vessels in protective positions once they cleared Naha's harbor.

When they were on the open sea, Shi Hua climbed the quarterdeck. Mateqai on her heels. "We will have that conversation now, Captain."

Biming stiffened at her use of his ship title, not his religious title. All the sailors froze in place at her disrespect. But then, all of the crew and officers of the Unbridled were Thief clergy and wardens.

He faced her, his cheeks rosy beneath his sparse facial hair. "I will not tolerate disrespect from a civilian."

"I'm showing the same respect that was given for my rank this morning," she replied coolly. She raised her right eyebrow, daring him to call her a liar in from of so many witnesses.

Biming nodded sharply. "Hadar, you have the helm until I return."

"Aye, sir." The priest from Hejaz glanced at them from the corners of his eyes, but he kept his attention on the ship's wheel. Po had said Hadar was quite intelligent and useful during the Siege of Tandor, but he gave no indication which way he might jump in this battle of wills.

"Is my quarters sufficient?" It was so rare for Biming to let his true emotions show on his face, but even his anger slipped past his quicksilver talent. If he believed he had a territorial advantage, he was sorely mistaken.

"Yes." She smiled and gestured at the stairs. "After you, Captain." At her mocking offer, unease flickered across his features.

The head of a nation's Temple was on equal status with the nation's leader. Po had said she would be his empress consort once he was crowned, which meant she would have equal authority on the Dragon Throne. And from the look on Biming's face, Po had told his old lover his plan.

Shi Hua followed Biming to his cabin. Two of his wardens and Mateqai attempted to enter, but she closed the door in their faces.

This needs to be a private conversation, Warden, she said silently by way of apology. She warded the cabin before she turned to Biming.

"May we speak plainly, human to human?"

He nodded slowly.

She cocked her head. "Is there a personal reason you tried to have Chief Justice Anthea killed this morning?"

"She's a potential danger to the human race—"

"I want the personal reason," she demanded. "You've spent sufficient time with Anthea to know she is honest to a fault. Are you that jealous of Po's attraction to her? Or am I your real target because I have replaced you in his bed?"

Biming's jaw dropped. "You think I am motivated by such petty—"

"Yes, I do." She smiled. "Assuming you're still human and not a demon wearing my mentor's skin."

He flushed at her assessment. "I am not jealous of you or Anthea. I am concerned because she fell through a demon portal—"

"And as she said under truthspell, the interaction between her spell,

Brother Jian's, and the skinwalkers caused the attempted portal to drop into an unknown dimension."

"But meeting Balance and Death—"

"Reverend Father, you read my report of what happened to me and High Sister Bertrice when the Orrin Temple of Balance was attacked last year." Shi Hua sighed and stared out the starboard window before her attention returned to Biming. "Was I also lying? Would you like to truthspell me now?"

His flush grew deeper, and he stared at the deck beneath his boots. "No, Your Imperial Highness."

So, Po had told Biming of his plan to name her empress consort.

"Anthea has been touched by the Twelve for whatever Their reasons," Shi Hua said softly. "Have you heard anything about a prophesy regarding her?"

"What?" His head jerked up, and shock filled his face. It was rather relaxing after his anger grating against her mental shields. "Foreknowledge is a very rare gift, and even then, it is not reliable. Where did you learn of such a thing?"

Shi Hua filed that bit of information away. The great Biming was fallible. Or was Anthea correct, and her own Reverend Mother was playing mind games with her?

"Let's just say with being on top of the Assassins Guild's list of targets, the chief justice and I compare notes on a regular basis," Shi Hua said. "But I have another question. Why is Reverend Ogusuku trying to undermine his own Temple of Balance two days after a demon attack within his own kingdom?"

Biming was silent for so long she wondered if he would refuse to answer her question. He finally sucked in a deep breath. "He told me he feared Fumiko wasn't ready for the responsibility, and Yoshiko's ill-health was compromising her judgement. And in Anthea's case, the sheer fact no one has ever come home after entering a demon portal was his main motivation. He believed the woman we think is Anthea is a demon."

"Do you agree with his reasoning?"

"Not after his performance this morning in the Temple of Balance." Biming shook his head. "I fear I did let my ego get in the way when it came to your judgement though, m'lady."

She cocked her head. "How so?"

"I still saw you as a novice of fourteen winters." He smiled sadly. "Instead of the woman you've become."

"I merely employed your teachings to protect the empire and the human race to the best of my ability, Reverend Father." Shi Hua bowed. "And I think Reverend Father Ogusuku severely underestimated the abilities of Fumiko to hold the seat of the Temple of Balance."

"She was rather prepared, wasn't she?" Biming chuckled but quickly sobered. "Maybe you are right. A bit of me is jealous of both Anthea and yourself. I still love Po."

Shi Hua shrugged. "I think he would be amenable to resuming your relationship with our return to Chengzhou, provided there was some discretion, of course."

"You would agree to such a thing?" Biming's shock seeped past his quicksilver talent. She didn't think she ever saw him lose control of his emotions, much less twice in the same day.

"I'm under no illusions." She smiled. "Our marriage is one of convenience. Po knows I'm fertile, but we are intimate only to produce his heirs. He has the advantage of having a fully trained former Light priestess at his beck and call. After eight years together, we trust each other to watch our respective backs.

She stepped closer to Biming. "However, you have lost a great deal of our trust with today's unnecessary political games at the Ryukyuan

Temple of Balance. It saddens us greatly we have greater trust and respect for foreigners, than our own countrymen, much less for someone we both love. Do you understand what I am saying?"

"Yes, m'lady," he said tightly.

"Good." She nodded sharply. "You will need to earn my trust again before you grace my husband's bed, and I will truthspell you before you do. Of course, that assumes Po will forgive you for your own part in Ogusuku's performance, as you called it."

That statement seemed to take Biming aback. "He knows?"

"I have no reason to lie to my husband." She lifted her right eyebrow. "Do you?"

Biming flushed crimson all the way to his ears. "No, m'lady. Would you care to truthspell me now?"

Shi Hua stepped back. "Not at this time. I'll let Chief Justice Anthea and High Brother Luc have that honor when we reach Jing."

She whirled on her boots and stalked from the Reverend Father's cabin. Either she nipped any potential problems with the home Temple of Thief, or she made an enemy of someone she considered her mentor, role model, and friend.

Chapter 11

I told Luc and our remaining wardens the full story of our encounter at the Ryukyuan Temple of Balance. The ship seemed terribly quiet now that Quan, Shi Hua, and their entire party were no longer onboard the *Mars Tranquilus*. I was terribly glad Luc sent Mateqai with them. We couldn't justify sending Long Feather, too, since no one was supposed to know Yin Li was a Love priestess, not Quan's concubine.

The five of us dined in the ship's guest cabin. Captain Titus offered his own cabin to us since Quan and his party were no longer using it. Luc declined on our behalf. I agreed. I'd had more than enough switching cabins with all the personal drama on the voyage west.

"I spoke directly with Reverend Father Jin," Luc said. "Apparently, Shi Hua tongue-lashed Reverend Father Biming privately as soon as we safely cleared Naha Harbor. She then reported her observations to Reverend Father Jin. Needless to say, he is rather appalled by Biming's behavior at the Ryukyuan Temple of Balance."

I poked at the shellfish and vegetables in my bowl with my eating sticks. As delicious as the scallops were compare to clams, I didn't have much of an appetite. The idea of Biming baring my neck was one thing. Betraying Quan and Shi Hua was another.

"What do we do?" Yar asked. The giant warden had been rather glum all afternoon. But then, Luc said Yin Shang had been rather put out that Yar didn't transfer to the *Unbridled*. The boy adored the warden, and he had been Yar's shadow for the last two months.

"Our mission is to keep Quan alive long enough to take the Dragon Throne." I shoved my bowl aside. "There's not much we can do if the Jing Temples have been corrupted."

Long Feather eyed my bowl before he looked at me with a pleading expression. I nodded. He seized the bowl and devoured the remainder of my meal. Jonata frowned at him, and from his wince, she kicked him beneath the table as well.

"Let him eat, Jonata," I ordered. "There's no sense in wasting food."

She lifted her chin. "Chief Warden Little Bear and Mistress Sivan ordered me to make sure you eat. You have a bad habit of skipping meals when there's a crisis."

Long Feather swallowed. "Why didn't you say something to me two months ago, instead of stomping on my toes now?"

Jonata's frown turned into a glare. "Because you've been assigned to Orrin longer than I have, and you should know your seat's habits, good or bad."

"I do know my seat's habits," he shot back. "I also know it's not a good idea to nag her when she's in a mood. If she hadn't eaten in several days, I wouldn't have finished her bowl. But when she comes home, raving about the foods she tried in these strange worlds she visited and bringing home the recipes, I'm not worried about her dying of starvation." He turned to me. "I want to try making this pizza you spoke of when it's my turn to cook the Rest Day evening meal."

Jonata rolled her eyes. "How in Balance are you so thin when you eat more than Yar?"

"Before this voyage, Sister Migina chased him constantly," Yar said dryly. "Running tends to work off one's meals."

Both Luc and I broke out in raucous laughter. Jonata snickered while Long Feather glared at Luc's warden.

Yar waited until our humor died before he said, "I am concerned about the political situation in Jing. If the Temples are already trying to sabotage their emperor-to-be, that only leaves the Guilds on the crown prince's side. I fear for your safety, High Brother, Chief Justice."

Luc and I exchanged looks. Yar rarely spoke, but when he did, it paid to listen.

I eyed my own wardens. "What is your analysis of the political situation?"

"Other than Long Feather's attempt to starve you?" Jonata said dryly.

I nodded.

"I agree with Yar." She shrugged. "Chengzhou is too far inland for a rapid escape. The Jing use signal fires much like the Plains Nations do. If the prince is assassinated despite our best efforts, I doubt our ability to get you and the high brother back to the *Mars Tranquilus*, even with your Thief talent."

"Thief talent? What Thief talent?" I blurted.

"Frankly, m'lady, you should be dead many times over." Jonata poked at the last scallop in her own bowl. "And you can resist the prince's talent, so yes, I believe you have a touch of Thief."

All of us watched Long Feather, waiting for his opinion. He sighed and set aside my bowl, which he had emptied.

"I know how this sounds, but for once, I wish Sister Migina were here." He shook his head. "I believe in the abilities of all the people at this table—"

"But?" I prompted.

"Even if we manage to keep the prince alive long enough to be crowned, that's no guarantee we'll make it out of Jing alive."

The normally ambitious and jovial warden's assessment sent a worm of worry squirming through my already upset stomach. It didn't help they all matched my own estimation of our situation.

Especially after the midday fiasco in Naha's Temple of Balance.

I turned to Luc. "Think this was another attempt to get rid of us?"

He pursed his lips before he shook his head. "Queen Teodora needed someone she trusted to get Quan home. Quan trusts you after you both shared valuable information over the last couple of years."

"And saved his buttocks in Tandor?" I said.

My sarcasm worked at breaking the growing tension inside our cabin. The other four chuckled.

"Temple seats have a little more authority and respect than nobles," Luc continued. "Not to mention, the queen's age dictates keeping Crown Princess Chiara nearby, for reasons that should be obvious after the death of Reverend Mother Yoshiko."

"Well, one of Queen Teodora's last instructions was that I and my party come home alive," I commented.

"Then we should abide by our queen's command," Luc said.

"Agreed." Jonata nodded sharply.

I raised my cup of Ryukyuan rice wine. "May the Twelve grant our success in this endeavor, my friends." The five of us clinked our cups together, and I prayed our gods listened to our plea.

Because I didn't know how else we would ever get back to Issura.

Chapter 12

Shi Hua suppressed a shiver as she disembarked the *Unbridled* on Po's arm. It would not do for the wife of the soon-to-be crowned emperor of Jing to show any emotion. Her fellow citizens waited to greet their new ruler at the end of the pier. They and the nobles would examine her for any possible weakness. Any little tidbit they could use against her, or worse Po.

Curiosity slammed against her mental shields. Both Reverend Father Jin and Brother Jian fed their energy into her to reinforce her own Light power. For a brief instant, she missed Brother Jeremy of Issura. They'd fought demons and conceived a child together, but there was a sweetness to him that had been reassuring, and she'd shared far more of herself with him than she did with her friends here in Jing. If she desired men, maybe she could have stayed in Issura.

But she wasn't afforded the luxury of choice. Po needed someone to watch his back all day, everyday. The only person who could do that would be the empress. It wasn't a role she desired, but her Temple training emphasized duty. Being his wife and the new empress of Jing meant fulfilling her duty of protecting humanity by keeping the Jing Empire politically stable in order to battle the latest demon incursions.

Warden Mateqai's presence at her back eased some of her tension. She'd come to depend on him during her time with the Issuran Temple of Light. As much as she wanted him to stay with her as part of her personal guard, she couldn't ask him to abandon his people, his culture, his position for a post in a foreign country half a world away from his home.

At the end of the gangplank, the Imperial Guard stood at attention. The twin lines ended with Duke Bao Lixin of Huang He and his retinue standing on the river shore. The duke was one of the many distant cousins who could possibly claim the throne should something happen to Po. However, both Reverend Father Jin of Light and Reverend Father Biming of Thief assured Po of this particular cousin's loyalty.

Shi Hua prayed they had actually truthspelled the duke and asked a justice to perform the interrogation. As she learned while serving in Issura, a good justice was needed to make sure the right questions were asked.

She studied the duke while she and her husband strode down the ceremonial line. He stood approximately two handspans taller than herself, but a handspan shorter than Po. The duke carried the sharp cheekbones and dimpled chin of the Bao linage, but his wide shoulders and bowlegged stance showed traits of the nobility in Huang He.

They reached the duke, who executed a proper bow. "The new emperor honors me and my people with his presence."

Before Po could respond, a flash of movement to her left caught her attention. A man dressed as a ducal guard raised something to his mouth.

Instinct kicked into motion. Shi Hua knocked Po to the carpet-covered ground, covered him with her body, and raised wards around them. An Imperial guardsman collapsed next to the pair. A dart with tiny brown sparrow feathers stuck from his cheek. The guardsman convulsed, and spit bubbled from his mouth.

Chaos and screaming erupted around them. Warden Mateqai,

Captain Huizhong, and the rest of the guards closed ranks to protect Po, but not before Brother Fa raced past them in his white tiger form.

From underneath Shi Hua, Po whispered, "For once, could you save my life without landing on top of me?"

"Forgive me for keeping you alive—"

The shouting abruptly stopped.

"What in the Twelve—" Po muttered.

She looked around them. Fa was frozen in mid-leap. Mateqai's sword had just cleared his scabbard. Jian had shoved aside an imperial guard as he followed Fa. The guard himself would fall on his rump when time resumed.

"My wards protected us from the chief justice's time freeze spell." Shi Hua rolled off her husband, jumped to her feet, and held out her hand to help him upright. "We need to get you out of here."

There's a carriage for you behind the duke's, Reverend Father Jin said silently. *High Brother Luc and Warden Yar are coming to escort you.*

We're taking the duke's carriage. Shi Hua concentrated, keeping her wards close about them while allowing freedom of movement. She drew her long knives from the voluminous sleeves of her formal mourning dress.

And she'd already stained the brand new outfit despite the protective rug on the ground.

She looked over her shoulder. Po had a pair of throwing knives in hand, and Luc and Yar approached at a rapid pace. "Follow me."

Not even a justice of Anthea's power and skills could keep the area between the pier and the surrounding offices and warehouses stopped in this moment of time forever. Shi Hua raced for the carriage decorated with Duke Lixin's pennants. She dodged curious merchants, dock workers, and fishwives, all of them frozen in the moment of the attack in front of them.

She reached the covered carriage and yanked on the lever. The door swung open. Thankfully, no one was inside. "Get in!"

Po did as she ordered with no argument. She ran to the driver, who stood by the lead horse of the quartet. After pulling the driver to the ground and dragging him out of the way, she clambered up onto the front seat and grabbed the reins.

Yar literally picked up Luc and lifted him and his crutches into the carriage before he joined Shi Hua on the driver's bench. But he stared at someone in the crowd.

"What's wrong?" Shi Hua demanded. "Another assassin?"

"I don't know." His brows drew into a single dark line. "We need to go, m'lady."

The rasp of Balance magic faded, and the screams of the crowd and shouts of the guards picked up where they left off.

Shi Hua flicked the reins. "Heeya!" The four matched horses galloped down the street, disregarding their original driver who ran after them for the first few blocks, shouting imprecations at Shi Hua. Reverend Father Jin whispered directions to the ducal palace in the back of her mind.

No, she responded crisply. *I'm heading for the Temple of Balance. It's easier to defend.*

Thank Light, the Reverend Father didn't question her choice.

She guided the horses into a right turn up the main thoroughfare of Huang He. Like most cities, the Temples were built on a north-south axis with Vintner and Death facing each other on the south end and Mother and Father on the north end. Local government offices continued past the Temples.

Luckily, the citizens recognized the ducal banners and Yar's Light warden uniform. They darted out of the path of the galloping horses. Maybe the Twelve guided her.

Relief trilled through Shi Hua at the site of the three-story pagodas of the main Temples. The home Temples were far more aesthetically pleasing than the harsh stone buildings in Issura. The main walls of each were painted in their order's color with the eaves painted in a coordinating color, so the resulting light and shadow gave the main structures the appearance of life and movement.

She slowed the horses and reined to stop in front of the black and white Temple of Balance. The two wardens at the main gate looked at each other, then at Shi Hua and Yar as the pair climbed down. Confusion marred both women's faces.

Shi Hua bowed slightly to them and tried to calm her racing heart. "I am Lady Shi Hua, wife of Crown Prince Bao Quan Po. I request the chief justice grant asylum for myself, my husband, and our retinue. There was an assassination attempt on the crown prince as we disembarked our ship."

The warden on the left bowed. "One moment, m'lady." She stepped inside the guardhouse and spoke with someone, but Shi Hua couldn't make out what was said. The warden came back a moment later.

"Your request is granted, my lady."

A third warden stepped out of the guardhouse on the other side of the wall. While she unlocked the gate, Yar knocked on the carriage door. Luc climbed out first and examined the area before he nodded.

Po exited the carriage, looking like he did this every day. However, Shi Hua could feel his anger. She didn't blame him. He'd taken approximately six steps on his native soil before someone tried to kill him.

As they entered the grounds of the Temple of Balance, Shi Hua wondered if she'd overestimated her ability to keep him alive long enough to take the Dragon Throne of Jing.

Chapter 13

Despite the healing, rest, and food after our last battle at sea with the skinwalkers, I couldn't hold the time freeze spell longer than a hundred heartbeats. It was long enough. Shi Hua and Yar sped away in a carriage as my strength gave out, and my spell collapsed. Jonata and Long Feather caught me when my knees gave out, and I started to go down on the pier.

"Get the justice back on the ship, Wardens!" Captain Titus bellowed from the deck above us.

My wardens half-guided and half-dragged me up the gangplank. Shouted orders punctuated the screams of fear from the civilians. Temple clergy and wardens poured from the three Jing ships that had come to our rescue before we reached the Kingdom of Ryukyu. Their running bootsteps along the pier bounced the gangplank. If it weren't for Jonata and Long Feather's firm grips on my arms, I would have fallen into the river.

And from the smell, it wouldn't be a pleasant experience at the best of times.

"What's happening?" I murmured as they settled me on the main deck.

A shriek of agony came from the direction of the duke's reception party. Or where the reception party had been standing when Shi Hua tackled Quan.

Which she wouldn't have done unless she spotted a threat.

"One of the duke's guards had what appeared to be a small blow pipe," Long Feather reported. "The dart hit one of the imperial guardsmen when Lady Shi Hua shoved the crown prince to the ground."

I wanted to know if Luc and Yar got the royal couple to safety, but I didn't dare reach out to my love. If he and his warden were in a battle to save Quan and Shi Hua, my interruption could distract them and turn the tide of their rescue. I also wanted to stand up to see what was happening onshore, but my leg joints and muscles refused to cooperate.

I sipped the water Little Squirrel brought to me until the hullaballoo on the docks dissipated. A voice called out from the pier in the Peaceful Sea trade tongue, "Permission to come aboard, Captain!"

Only then did I realize the crew had pulled up the gangplank behind me and my wardens.

"One moment!" Titus shouted back. He strode over to me. "The Jing Reverend Father of Light and Duke Lixin wish to come aboard and speak with you, m'lady."

I nodded despite the vertigo still plaguing me. Little Squirrel took the cup I handed back to her, and my wardens helped me to a vertical position.

Once the gangplank was in place, Reverend Father Jin and the duke came aboard with one warden and one guard.

The Jing priest bowed to me. "Thank you for your assistance. We would not have caught the assassin without you freezing the entire area between piers and the warehouses."

"Did he carry poison in his tooth or on his person?" I asked. "And be careful with any weapons he may have on him. The Assassins Guild likes playing with poison a little too much."

Duke Lixin nodded. "Unfortunately, this isn't our first encounter with the Assassins Guild, Lady Justice. Sister Xin Yan of Love was disguised as one of my daughters as a precaution. She is a most powerful mover. The shriek you may have heard was her removal of the assassin's poison tooth."

"What about the crown prince and his wife?"

The two men exchanged rather bemused looks before the duke said, "Our new empress stole my personal carriage, two of your Light personnel, and took her husband to our Temple of Balance."

"She deemed it the best fortified." Reverend Father Jin shook his head. "However, nearly all of our Temples in the empire are built in the same basic style, using similar materials."

"It's not the style or the building material," I said. "It's the spells she sought."

"I don't understand." The Reverend Father looked even more perplexed.

"When you allowed her temporary assignment to Orrin's Temple of Light, she and my junior, Justice Yanaba, worked on ways to supplement and compliment each other's skills and techniques." I smiled graciously at the two men. "Our century reprieve from demon attacks has made all of the human race rather lax. We've lost much knowledge, not to mention we need to develop new strategies for dealing with both the demons and the human renegades."

The duke scowled at me. "Are you saying Jing is not prepared to fight?"

"None of us are truly prepared, Your Grace," I said softly. "Issura lost an entire city last year. And you've lost your previous emperor. Other nations around the Peaceful Sea have losses over the past year, great and small. I merely stated an unfortunate fact. No offense was meant."

My speech seemed to mollify the duke's ego. He nodded. "I

apologize for jumping to conclusions, Lady Justice. I fear everyone in Jing is on edge due to the attack in Chengzhou."

"There may be ways to alleviate both of our concerns and share knowledge," I said. "Before her passing, Reverend Mother Yoshiko of Balance in the Kingdom of Ryukyu mentioned when she was a novice, there was an exchange program among the nations on this side of the Peaceful Sea. Perhaps we could restart such a program. Learn more from each others' experiences. And not limit it to Temple personnel only."

My last suggestion piqued the duke's interest.

He nodded slowly. "Your ideas are something to consider. However, you must make the proposal. I fear my cousin may not be in mood to hear it from me. Not when the assassin was part of my guard."

"I have come to serve, Your Grace." I inclined my head. "Your cousin and my queen have spoken. They've come to realize they have common enemies, and they need to work together."

"You speak wisely, Lady Justice." Duke Lixin returned the gesture.

"In the meantime, we should see to your future emperor and his wife's safety," I added. All I could sense was concern from both men, though I couldn't tell if it were for Quan and Shi Hua personally, their nation as a whole, or simply their own positions within the empire.

Both men turned to disembark the *Mars Tranquilus*. I took a step to follow them when Captain Titus stepped closer.

"M'lady, I would feel better if a few of my crew accompanied you," he murmured in Issuran. "I mean no disrespect to your wardens, but the numbers are not on our side."

"No," I whispered. "Make any trades with the local merchants as we planned. Have your ship ready to leave at a moment's notice. And if I tell you to set sail—" I tapped my temple. "—you will do so with no argument. I will feed you as much information as I can—"

"Before you die?" he growled.

"If it comes to that, my friend, then yes."

Titus's eyes widened at my term for him.

"We've been through too much together the past two winters to be otherwise," I added.

He broke etiquette and grabbed me in a tight bear hug. His affection rolled over my psyche. I found I didn't mind his gesture quite so much.

"You need to come back here alive, Anthea." His words and breath brushed my ear. "And bring Luc and your wardens with you, so we can all go home together."

We parted, and I nodded. The lump in my throat wouldn't allow any words past it.

Little Squirrel and Sea Wolf had collected our bags from our cabin. They and another crew member named Octopus carried them down the pier.

At the bottom of the gangplank, Mateqai joined us. His irritation rubbed along my psyche.

"I did not intentionally interfere with your duties," I said.

He sighed and looked away for a moment before he turned back to me. "I don't think there's a warden alive who can keep up with Lady Shi Hua." He chuckled in a self-deprecating manner. "Though the Twelve know I've tried."

"She was used to her independence," I said. "She's still adjusting to her new role as well."

Duke Lixin and his family took the carriage meant for the imperial couple. A third carriage was for Captain Huizhong and the rest of Quan's guards. A fourth was for the Issuran party.

After the crewmembers of the *Mars Tranquilus* loaded our bags into the overhead compartment, both Little Squirrel and Sea Wolf also gave me and the wardens tight hugs.

Octopus made the gesture of good luck. "May Thief grant you good fortune, Lady Justice."

"Thank you." I climbed into the carriage along with the three wardens. Reverend Father Jin and a good number of the clergy and wardens with him formed an escort along with members of the Huang He Temples for the three remaining carriages.

No one in my carriage spoke. There was nothing to say. We'd had too many close calls since we left Orrin two months ago. We'd barely been in Jing a few candlemarks before there was yet another assassination attempt on Quan.

I needed to ask the chief justice of Balance here in Huang He if I could observe her interrogation of the assassin. This matter wasn't something she could leave to her junior justices. But I would have to couch my request with some delicacy given I was a visitor here.

But having a living member of the Assassins Guild to question wasn't an opportunity I could pass up.

Chapter 14

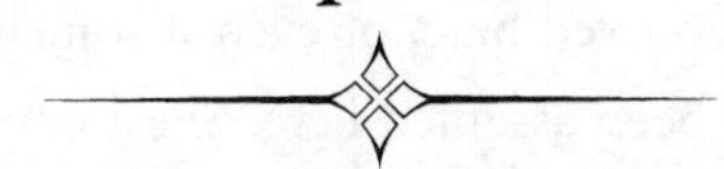

Shi Hua paced in the Balance receiving room. It was larger than the one in Orrin's sister Temple, but then, they were also on the second story of the pagoda. The pale wooden walls were oiled and polished to a high shine. Beautifully carved chairs and side tables covered in black lacquer lined the walls. The austere design made the large room feel even larger, which meant it was perfect for pacing.

The buildings on the north and south sides of the pagoda housed clergy, wardens, and staff. The stables, workshops, and outdoor training area sat on the west side of the complex.

Since Huang He was a major port, much like Issura's capital of Standora, their Temple of Balance would be just as busy. Centers of wealth tended to attract those who tried to scam and steal even in the best of times. Since Jing's population was also much larger than Issura's, they needed more justices.

While most Temples in Jing used stone or brick for their pagodas, the coastal areas built with wood. They often had to deal with the remnants of the same storms that roared over the Kingdom of Ryukyu and the Fire Islands during late autumn.

The odd combination of familiar and not familiar troubled her. She was homesick . . . for Issura. But then, she'd spent over a third of her life there.

One of the junior justices had their party escorted here since court was in session and Chief Justice Li Chun was training her most recent initiate. A member of the Balance staff served them tea before she retreated and left them alone. None of them dared to touch the cups, much less the drink.

Shi Hua had never been to Huang He before now. She didn't know any of the clergy who lived here, or even if someone she knew from her novice days had been assigned here. She'd never met Duke Lixin though Po had spoken well of him. And worst of all, it bothered her she no longer felt safe with any Temple personnel outside of the people she knew personally. But if she had to choose a Temple in an emergency, Balance topped her list.

"My dear, you made the best decision you could under the circumstances," Po said. "Quit fretting."

"It's a bad habit she picked up from a certain justice." Luc wore a wry smile.

"I've noticed she's picked up a great many habits from a certain justice," Po replied.

Shi Hua decided to ignore their jibes and focused on Yar. "Who or what did you see in the crowd, Warden?"

The same uncomfortable expression as before crossed his face. "I thought I spotted Skoloti markings on the scabbard of a person in the crowd."

"Skoloti?" Po straightened in his chair, his manner intent.

Yar nodded. "Assuming I remember my grandfather's lessons accurately. The Rus are descended from the Skandza, the Themiscyreians, and the Skoloti."

"The Skoloti trade with the Xiongnu Confederation," Po said. "With the demon attack on the Khan, they also would have sent aid."

Shi Hua understood Yar's suspicion. "But why would a Skoloti be this far south in Jing? They're nomads, much like the Northern Long Continent's Plains Nations."

"For that matter, so are the tribes of the Xiongnu Confederation," Luc offered. "But if this person was a spy, why advertise their affiliation?"

"Unless they were exiled," Po suggested. "Neither the Xiongnu or any other non-Skoloti people would take them in. They could simply be searching for a new place to call home."

"Or they could be an assassin," Shi Hua bit out.

Yar chuckled. "It's not like a Skoloti could blend in with the Jing population the way the Xiongnu could. The Assassins Guild tries very hard not to call attention to themselves. Like using Duke Lixin's guards."

"That's one of the lovely things about Anthea's vision." Shi Hua sighed. "Everyone has the same skin color, eye color, and hair color to her."

"It's not a perfect way to look at the world," Luc said. "There are things she misses."

"But there's much she catches with her sight we can't," Shi Hua protested.

"You mean like when she knows someone is lying without using a truthspell?"

"And what lie did she catch you in, High Brother?" Po smirked.

"Stop!" Shi Hua snapped. "Both of you! We have enough problems without your manure flinging." She shook her head. "Light help me, is this what you two were like during the Siege of Tandor?"

"Actually, we were too busy getting tortured," Luc said dryly. "Then the demons distracted us."

"Gah!" Shi Hua threw up her arms. "If I were in Anthea's position, I would have struck you both with lightning!"

At the polite knock on the door, Yar slipped one of his knives from its scabbard and opened the door a crack.

"Reverend Father Jin and Duke Lixin along with the Issuran ambassador have arrived," a feminine voice said in the trade tongue. "The Chief Justice has been informed of their arrival and will join you shortly."

"Thank you, Warden." Yar nodded to his opposite before closing the door.

"Thank you for not stabbing my cousin or the Reverend Father of Light." Sarcasm dripped from Po's voice.

"My dear, the Issuran ambassador and her companions have been tasked by their queen with keeping you alive." Shi Hua crossed her arms. "And your behavior is unbecoming in a Jing emperor."

Po inclined his head, the gold beads swinging at the end of his moustache. "You are right, my wife. Please forgive my bad mood. I do not like being a target."

The door to the receiving room swung open. "Now, you know how I've felt for the last two years," Anthea quipped.

She strode into the room as if it were her own receiving room back in Orrin. Reverend Father Jin and Duke Lixin followed her inside. However, none of them looked half as upset as Mateqai.

He stomped up to Shi Hua. "With all due respect, m'lady, I thought we had an understanding you would not scamper off like the chief justice now that you are the crown prince's wife until we recruited adequate personal guards for you here in Jing."

Anthea leaned closer to Luc and said in Issuran, "Have you ever noticed whenever someone says 'with all due respect', they are never respectful?"

"Considering how many times you've used that phrase with me—" Po started.

"Please use your manners, my husband, Chief Justice," Shi Hua said in Jing. "While I realize you both use black humor to deal with violence against yourselves, now is neither the time nor the place."

"Yes, m'lady," the pair answered at the same time in Jing. However, they both wore impish grins.

Duke Lixin knelt the appropriate distance from Po. "I pray you were unharmed, Your Majesty. I failed in my duty to you. I will accept any punishment you deem necessary." He glanced up at Po. "Please spare my family," Lixin finished in a whisper.

Po regarded him for a long moment. "You will be truthspelled here and now, my cousin. Your cooperation will be sufficient payment."

Her husband's terms seemed to take the duke by surprise, but he ducked his head, and his relief washed through the room.

Until Po added, "High Brother Luc, Chief Justice Anthea, would you do me the honor of interrogating my cousin?"

Chapter 15

I wanted to smack Quan below his well-oiled top knot. What was he trying to prove? Even I understood he needed to build a consortium amongst the Jing nobles to seal his claim to the imperial throne. But he'd just insulted the Jing Temples along with the nobility.

In fact, Reverend Father Jin was boiling mad beneath his calm exterior. Balance only knew how the chief justice of Huang He would react to a foreign justice stepping outside of her jurisdiction, even if it was at the request of her nation's ruler.

Maybe there was a way to mollify egos and save the situation.

I cleared my throat and said in my best Jing, "May we wait until the chief justice of Huang He can join us, Your Majesty? It would be best to share our experience and knowledge concerning the Assassins Guild with her and Reverend Father Jin at the same time." Thankfully, I didn't stumble too badly over my pronunciation. Two solid months of practice during the voyage across the Peaceful Sea helped immensely.

To my own relief, Quan nodded. "Please rise and take a seat, cousin. No sense in being uncomfortable while we wait."

Duke Lixin stood, but he looked at Shi Hua with a bit of worry. "M'lady?" He gestured at the chair next to Quan's.

She dimpled and turned on her charm. "May we not stand on ceremony for the short time we are in Huang He, cousin? I have been cooped up on ships far too long. I need to get my land legs back."

Luc and Quan both looked at me, my love with amusement and the crown prince with a touch of irritation.

"Your habits have corrupted my bride, Chief Justice." But there was no real bite to Quan's words.

I shrugged. "I believe I've corrupted her just enough to keep you alive, Your Majesty. However, I'm slightly perturbed she has already stained one of her mourning dresses. Her trousseau is only a few days old."

An alarmed expression spread over the duke's face. "The bride's family should handle such matters, not an Issuran justice."

"Her family wasn't available, Your Grace," I said. "And the money came from a Thief gaming tournament I won the same night Emperor Bao Chengwu and his sons were assassinated. The Twelve are looking out for Lady Shi Hua, and it was my honor to provide her trousseau. She is a sister to me. Maybe even more so than my fellow justices."

"And as I said, the lady voluntarily left Temple service so His Majesty can reintroduce Light blood in the line of the Bao family," Reverend Father Jin added.

None too gently either.

Bright orange highlighted the duke's skin as he realized he had insulted me and my friendship with his new empress. "I beg your forgiveness, Chief Justice, Lady Shi Hua. Since the lady is now married to my cousin, and since you consider her a sister, you are both family."

The receiving room door swung open again. This time, the chief justice of Huang He entered on the arm of her chief warden. She was tiny, even compared to Shi Hua or Jonata. Her hood was pushed back to display her blue hair in a complicated braid design. Her chief warden wore leggings, a padded vest, and a tunic similar in style to those worn by my own wardens. However, he wore a long coat over them, and his sword and scabbard hung from his belt.

"Welcome to Huang He, Crown Prince Po," she announce to the room in general in the trade tongue. "I am Chief Justice Li Chun, and this is Chief Warden Junfeng. We come to serve."

Quan went quickly through the rest of the introductions. The chief justice smiled when he came to me.

"I am honored to meet you, sister. Your information and Lady Shi Hua's experience in Issura have been most helpful in defending our nation."

I bowed even though she couldn't see me, and I had to quell the urge make light of our demon encounters. But in doing so, I became starkly aware I should be dead many times over.

"I am glad our small contributions have been helpful."

"The crown prince's attacker has been brought to the Balance gaol," she said. "We owe you for your quick thinking. This is the first time I'm aware of where a member of the Assassins Guild has been captured."

"I wish I was as quick thinking in Issura," I said. "We had far too many members of the Assassins Guild slip through our grasp."

"Do not belittle your abilities and insight, Chief Justice," Chief Justice Li Chun said. "May we consult before I interrogate him? You have much more experience with the Assassins Guild than I do. Any insights would be most helpful."

"I would be honored to assist you, Chief Justice." I wanted to sag in relief. I didn't have to cajole, beg, or threaten to be involved in the assassin's questioning.

"Reverend Father Biming and I will also attend the interrogation," Reverend Father Jin stated.

She cocked her head in the direction of his voice. "While you have that right, Reverend Father, I would ask that neither of you interfere in my duty. I do not wish for any questions about how my Temple has handled this investigation."

And there went any feeling of good will I had for Li Chun. Was she involving me so she had someone to blame if something went wrong?

"Chief Justice Li Chun, I hope you truly want Chief Justice Anthea's insight," Quan said. "I already had an issue with another nation's Reverend Father of Thief attempting to use her to undermine his own Reverend Mother of Balance."

Li Chun sighed heavily. "If you are referring to the incident upon Reverend Mother Yoshiko's recent death in the Kingdom of Ryukyu, I've already read the dispatch." She held up a hand. "Before you ask, it was relayed by distance speaker since Reverend Mother Fumiko has filed a formal complaint for all the Balance Temple heads to review."

Part of me wanted to cheer over Fumiko holding her ground against Reverend Father Ogusuku, but it would be unseemly for the Issuran ambassador to do so.

"Chief Justice Anthea, our own Reverend Mother in Chengzhou wishes to speak with you before she votes," Li Chun continued.

Well, that was a nice little twist. "She wants formal testimony from me?" I asked.

"Perhaps." Li Chun pressed the wrist of her chief warden. He led her to an unoccupied chair near me, and she sat.

"I was merely to relay the message when you arrived in Huang He," she continued. "However, I had assumed we would meet at Duke Lixin's reception for our new emperor tonight. We both hold our mission close to our hearts. We pray you will not hold our Reverend Father of Thief's bad manners and poor judgment against the Jing Temple of Balance."

"Neither Reverend Father Biming nor myself will interfere with your duties, Chief Justice Li Chun," Reverend Father Jin said.

"Have I and the Reverend Father reassured you, Your Majesty?" she asked.

The tension between Quan and the head of Jing's Temple of Light was a palpable thing. It felt as if one wrong word or gesture would shatter the very air in the room.

"Your wisdom and graciousness exceed my expectations, Chief Justice." Quan stroked his beard. "However, I pray to the Twelve that you understand why I must reserve my judgment on the situation."

A flash of humor quirked Li Chun's lips. "Given the circumstances of your ascension to the Dragon Throne, I would expect no less. And I must add it relieves me to know our new emperor has the patience to learn all the facts of a matter before passing judgement."

So, Li Chun was in a similar position to mine, dancing on the edge of a blade in trying to keep Jing intact and stable. And while I was glad Quan knew how to play the long game, I worried he would overlook the disaster in Ryukyu due to his affection for Biming.

Chapter 16

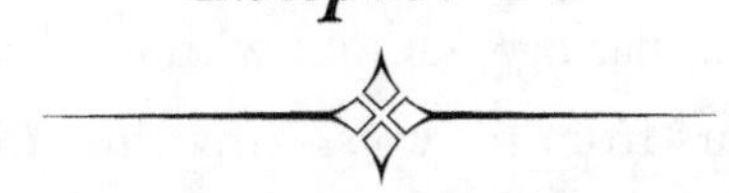

"Chief Justice Li Chun, may I also observe the prisoner's interrogation?" Shi Hua could read Anthea's body language well enough to know she wasn't entirely comfortable with her role as a consultant. After the fiasco in Naha, Shi Hua didn't blame her friend. No doubt she feared this was another attempt to increase political power and influence within the Temples, sacrificing her in the process.

The Huang He seat of Balance cocked her head. "Most nobles and royalty only want to see the execution phase in a case like this."

"My lady wife was a priestess of Light," Po said. "I would appreciate you indulging her."

"Lady Shi Hua supplemented my staff at the Orrin Temple of Light with Reverend Father Jin's permission," Luc added, speaking for the first time. "I can vouch for her behavior and character."

Li Chun leaned closer to where Anthea stood. "What say you, Chief Justice Anthea?"

A startled expression crossed her features at someone, a justice foreign to her no less, actually wanted her opinion. Shi Hua bit her lower lip to keep from laughing. Now would definitely not be the time.

"Lady Shi Hua's manners and conduct were exemplary in my court," Anthea said. "I found her insights invaluable during investigations, and her fighting skills are superb whether facing a demon, a skinwalker, or a human foe. She will not interfere in your case unless her husband's assailant somehow gets free and causes mayhem."

Li Chun chuckled. "In such a case, I would hope both of you would allow my wardens to handle such things."

Po and Luc roared with laughter at her statement. Even Mateqai and Yar smirked.

"Would you mind sharing your joke with me?" Li Chun asked.

Po wiped the tears from his eyes. "Any time there was trouble in Orrin over the past two years, Anthea and Shi Hua would be in the middle of it. They were usually saving everyone else."

"It's not like we caused the trouble, my husband," Shi Hua gently chided.

Li Chun covered her mouth to hide what Shi Hua was fairly certain was a smile.

"In fact, the trouble went out of their way to find us," Anthea added.

"Then I have the right people to flush out any problems," Li Chun said.

Duke Lixin cleared his throat. "My staff has prepared rooms for you and your retinue, Your Majesty. However, I understand if you wish to remain at the Temple of Balance."

Po hesitated for a miniscule moment, something Shi Hua doubted anyone but his most immediate confidants would have noticed.

"Would you be amenable to your staff and guards being truthspelled prior to us accepting your hospitality?" she said. "My request is not a reflection on you, Your Grace, but based on renegades infiltrating the Jing embassy in Issura."

"Also, my original second was a renegade." Luc gestured at his left leg. "I had no idea of his true allegiance until my predecessor was murdered and I lost my foot. Knowledge had to teach me a hard lesson."

"Our other concern is the Bao line specifically being targeted,"

Anthea said. "Even if the crown prince were not staying with you, I would recommend you still have everyone in your household, family, staff, and guards, be truthspelled for their own protection."

Parental worry slammed into Shi Hua's psyche. Anthea's warning caused the duke to reconsider his own wife and sons' safety.

He nodded slowly. "You all speak wisely. I acquiesce to Lady Shi Hua's request."

Shi Hua was about to volunteer to go to the duke's manse when Luc said, "I will take care of this detail, Your Majesty." He climbed to his foot and balanced on his crutches. "If I may borrow one or two of your priests, Reverend Father, it would speed the process."

"I would recommend Brother Jian," Shi Hua said. "We were in the same novice class, and I would trust him with my life."

"Of course," Reverend Father Jin murmured. "Do you have a request for a second and third assistant to the high brother?"

"I'll abide by your recommendation for an additional priest or priestess from Light." A mischievous smile lit Luc's face. "I'd like to solicit Brother Fa's assistance as well. The Wildling's second form would make even an experienced assassin think twice before engaging him."

"I can see why our new emperor requested you to accompany him back to Jing." The Reverend Father turned to Li Chun. "I pray to Light we don't fill your cells, Chief Justice."

She sighed again. "Unfortunately, they've been full for the last two months. Frightened people do very stupid things."

Everyone in the room murmured in agreement.

She stood and held out her left hand. Her chief warden took it and wrapped her fingers around his elbow. "I understand none of you has touch your tea. Chief Justice Anthea, if one or two of your wardens would like to observe our kitchen staff as a precaution, I would totally understand your reasons for doing so."

"If it were only my wellbeing, I would accept the word of a sister for her Temple," Anthea said.

"But it's not only your wellbeing, which is why I make the offer," Li Chun responded. "I would prefer extra attention on those under my command. I don't assume I'm infallible. The last thing I wish is for the emperor to be harmed because I allowed my pride to get in the way of my duty."

"As would I," Anthea said.

"Warden Mateqai, please take Warden Jonata with you to the Balance kitchen," Shi Hua ordered. He opened his mouth to protest. She knew he would, but she held up her hand to stop him.

"We won't start the interrogation without the two of you. I promise," she said. "Right now, the crown prince's protection takes priority. That means he needs to eat food we know isn't poisoned. You've been testing my meals for the past year. Chief Justice Li Chun's staff will be more comfortable with wardens watching them. Captain Huizhong and his men can certainly keep an eye on my husband while you and Warden Jonata check his meal."

A sheepish smile tilted Mateqai's lips. "You do understand my concerns after all the attempts on your life."

"And I have the same concerns for my husband after all the attempts on his life." Shi Hua smiled in return.

"Now that we know everyone is concerned for everyone else, perhaps we could get started on our respective tasks," Anthea said.

For some strange reason, the familiarity of being involved in an attempted murder investigation relieved Shi Hua's anxiety. She just wished the intended victim wasn't her groom of less than a month.

Chapter 17

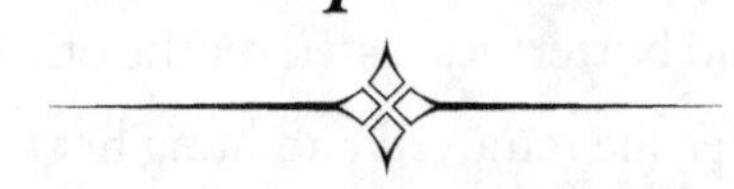

Long Feather accompanied me to Chief Justice Li Chun's private office as did her own chief warden Junfeng. Her personal assistant waited outside of her door.

"Do you have a tea preference, Chief Justice Anthea?" Li Chun asked.

"Black Jing, if you have it," I replied.

"Are you teasing me?" she asked.

"No, Lady Justice, she is not," Long Feather blurted. "The entire Orrin Temple of Balance knows not to bother her before she's had the first cup of Jing black in the morning."

Li Chun laughed while Junfeng frowned at my warden.

"I hope you'll pardon Warden Long Feather." I eyed the Huang He warden. "I encourage my wardens to state their honest opinions."

"About your personal habits, Chief Justice?" Junfeng appeared puzzled.

"There's worse things he could have told you," I quipped.

"Black tea then please, Lu Zhi, and some treats," Li Chun ordered her assistant, who scampered down the hallway. "Let us talk, sister."

The two wardens moved to follow us into the office.

"We can manage this discussion alone, wardens," Li Chun said. No irritation in her voice, but she clearly would brook no argument.

I accompanied her into her office, and she firmly closed the door behind us. Her personal taste was similar to mine, but the room seemed far less crowded than my office in Orrin. Scrolls and books neatly stacked on shelves. Hooks along the wall for weapons and robes. Her stamp set sat in a lovely jade box on top of her lacquered desk. Matching chairs sat on the door side of her desk while a more ornate chair decorated with silver flowers and butterflies rested on the other side. That was the chair she claimed after she removed and hung her sword harness.

"Have a seat," she said. Wards sprang to life, tickling my skin. "Would you mind terribly if we forego titles while we speak? I swear I'm dehydrated from the short conversation in the receiving room."

I laughed. "You are a justice after my own heart, Li Chun."

She smiled. "I admit I wanted to gain your acquaintance. As someone who gained her sight, why are you still a part of Balance?"

If I had any doubts about every Temple of Balance knowing about me, they were immediately quashed. Of course, she was curious.

"Is this a legal question?" I asked.

"Actually, yes." Li Chun rested her hands in her lap. "It's been a question among the Reverend Mothers around the World. There's never been someone born blind who regained their sight. There's been cases where female clergy have lost their sight long after birth and were healed. But your case is highly unusual."

"And what do my sisters outside of Issura say about me gaining sight?"

"The question of your status is fairly evenly split between three lines of analysis," Li Chun said. "Some believe once Balance has claimed you, you cannot leave Temple service."

"Which is my Reverend Mother's opinion." I managed to keep my bitterness from my voice.

"Some believe you should have been released from service once you gained your sight," Li Chun continued.

"And the third?" I prompted.

"You may be the first of a thirteenth deity."

The idea sent a shiver of dread through me. Such an idea would be considered heresy by the more orthodox members of our order.

"What is the reasoning of the third group?" I asked.

"Because the Wildling God is substantially different when compared to the other Eleven." She hesitated for a moment. "I apologize for disturbing you, Anthea. That was not my intent."

"Did you expect me to accept such a sacrilegious theory?"

She smiled. "Either you are as gifted at dissembling as a Thief priest, or you're not as full of yourself as the rumors would say."

"We are justices," I said as calmly as I could manage. "We should be dealing with facts, not hearsay and gossip."

She laughed. "Well, one of the rumors is true. Your logic is impeccable."

A knock on the office door interrupted us. Li Chun lowered her wards and called out, "You may enter."

Her assistant entered, a scowl on her face. A scowl I recognized.

"My apologies for Warden Long Feather's behavior, Mistress Lu Zhi." I inclined my head. "There's been several attempts to poison me since I was named as Orrin's chief justice."

"Your warden was performing his duties, Chief Justice." She carefully poured tea into the two cups. Orange steam rose into the air, fading to yellow and green before it fully dissipated.

"Lu Zhi is irritated the wardens have switched from protection mode to everyone's guilty until proven otherwise over the last two months," Li Chun said.

"Then the last two years with my wardens would have driven you absolutely mad, mistress," I murmured as she handed me a warm cup. For once, a Balance staff member didn't assume I was blind.

Lu Zhi giggled. "Last spring's new edict has made up for the constant suspicion, m'lady."

Li Chun grimaced while her assistant pressed the second cup into the chief justice's palms. "Yes, the Reverend Mothers alter their stance on relationships just as I'm entering the final change."

"M'lady, your cycles haven't stopped," Lu Zhi said. "There is still the possibility if you would pursue it."

It was my turn to laugh. "You sound like my head of household."

"You haven't pursued the edict's allowance?" Surprise flavored Li Chun's question.

"I can pursue it all I want," I said dryly. "However, all the pursuit in the world won't change the fact I'm infertile thanks to the first poisoning attempt."

"My apologies, Anthea," Li Chun said. "We didn't mean to step into your personal affairs."

"Actually, it's quite nice to have an honest conversation." I eyed the plates Lu Zhi sat in front of me and Li Chun. The fare seemed to be various dried fruits and balls of cooked dough, though each plate contained a dough ball with a bite missing. "And our wardens could have simply eaten an entire dough ball."

"But they needed to leave proof they checked the food." Li Chun smiled.

"My wardens and High Brother Luc's took a bite out of every single almond pastry on the serving platter one night."

Both the chief justice and her assistant laughed.

"Thank you, Lu Zhi," Li Chun said. "I'll call for you if we need anything further."

"Yes, Lady Justice." The girl bowed to both of us before she departed the office.

Once the door closed, Li Chun reestablished her wards.

"You are loose in your standards with your staff," I said. "It's wonderful to see another chief justice treating their people like human beings."

"There's far too much pressure on the Temples in Jing at the moment." She took a sip of her tea. "There are those who blame us for Emperor Chengwu's death. Our Reverend Mother understands there needs to be some levity so our personnel don't collapse with physical or emotional problems."

I paused in taking a sip of my own tea. "Is that why the crown prince was escorted to a receiving room?"

"That was for his own safety," she answered. "I didn't want to advertise his presence in my Temple." She sighed and sipped her tea. "Shall we go over any additions to the interrogation of our failed assassin?"

I nodded. But my nerves didn't like Li Chun's new information one bit. If Quan couldn't win over the populace along with the nobility, the Temples, and the guilds, he wouldn't survive long enough to reach Chengzhou.

Chapter 18

Shi Hua perched on her chair in the receiving room and sipped tea while she watched Po pace the room. "You are going to wear out your boot soles, my husband."

He paused and glared at her, though his anger was directed elsewhere. "I don't like being restricted in my actions. I feel like I'm the one under arrest."

"Things have changed for both of us," she said softly.

He crossed the room, sat next to her, and leaned close. "I'm sorry I dragged you into this farce."

She chuckled. "I seem to recall being the one who said yes every time you asked something of me."

"And yet, you've asked so little in return," he said.

"I came to serve." She cupped his cheek. "I will continue to do so with my last breath. I just wish—"

He laid his right palm against her hand on his face. "You wish what?"

"That I loved you in the way you deserve."

Bitter laughter poured from him. "If I got what I deserved, a skin-walker would have flayed me long before now."

She shook her head at his dark humor. Maybe that was the reason she was attracted to Anthea. The justice was the feminine aspect of her husband. She and Po had terrible childhoods that scarred their hearts and minds. Shi Hua set aside her tea cup. Unfortunately, there were things in life she could not change, and she'd always had trouble accepting those.

At the knock on the door, all of Po's guards jumped. Captain Huizhong cracked the door open, then stepped out of the way as Mateqai and Jonata entered the room. Both wardens bowed to Shi Hua.

"They're ready for the interrogation down in the gaol, m'lady," Mateqai said. "And Mistress Yin Li and her son have arrived. May they enter, Your Majesty?"

"Of course," Po said.

Captain Huizhong opened the door once again. Yin Li entered. Little Yin Shang raced around her and launched himself into Po's arms.

"Are you all right, Prince Po? We saw my cousin push you to the ground, and Justice Anthea froze everyone but you and Shi Hua! I wanted to help, but Mother made me stay with her while Yar left with you!" The boy gasped after his breathless recitation.

"I am fine, Master Yin Shang." Po smiled at the child. "As is Lady Shi Hua."

Yin Shang turned and bowed to her. "I beg forgiveness for not greeting you properly, my lady."

"Actually, I am quite glad you and Mistress Yin Li are here." Shi Hua rose. "I must perform an errand. Could you please assist Captain Huizhong in guarding the prince while your mother entertains him? I will return shortly."

"Are you truthspelling the bad man for Justice Anthea?" he asked with the bluntness of innocence.

"No, she and I will be acting as witnesses while Chief Justice Li Chun questions him."

Yin Shang nodded sharply. "I will be here if you need assistance, my lady."

You all indulged my child far too much during our voyage home, Yin Li said silently though her mental voice held a touch of humor.

I wish many of our fellow humans had your son's enthusiasm for duty, Shi Hua replied.

"High Brother Luc and his party will be returning once they truthspell Duke Lixin's staff," she added out loud. "If he clears everyone at the manse, the crown prince's party will be staying there. If not—" She shrugged. "—we may want to purchase some hammocks for the Balance receiving room."

She turned to Jonata. "Warden, would you mind—"

The Issuran woman inclined her head. "I would be happy to assist Master Yin Shang in protecting the crown prince."

"Thank you." Shi Hua returned her gesture before she charged out the door, Mateqai on her heels.

"M'lady, may we speak privately when you have the opportunity?" he murmured.

Shi Hua slowed her pace and switched to the Issuran language. "May I ask what this is about?"

"Would you accept my service as your guardsman?" His request came out in a rush as if he feared she would say no.

"You want to leave Temple service?" She didn't dare turn to look at him. She'd come to depend on him while in Orrin, but asking him to leave his homeland was more than she could demand of him. "Have you spoken with High Brother Luc about this?"

"I have, m'lady. He—"

They passed a Balance staff member who stopped and bowed. Shi Hua inclined her head.

Mateqai waited until the woman had continued on her way and was out of hearing range. "Both he and Chief Justice Anthea have already given me their blessing to ask you. I expected to do so once we had a private moment tonight. The renegades had other ideas."

While she secretly hoped to keep him with her, she knew it for the fantasy it was. She'd never experienced the loyalty of the wardens until she was assigned to the Orrin Temple of Light. She'd left Jing as Po's personal bodyguard mere candlemarks after she took her final vows as a full-fledged priestess. Mateqai had gone above and beyond in protecting her. Especially with Brother Jeremy's emotional problems and High Brother Luc's self-medication after the horrors both men experienced last year.

"I don't like leaving him with only Warden Yar," Shi Hua replied.

"Frankly, m'lady, if we all survive our journey to Chengwu and your husband's coronation, I do not fear for the high brother's safety on the return trip to Issura. He and the chief justice earned the loyalty of the crew of the *Mars Tranquilus*. Yar will have plenty of assistance."

"What about Chief Warden Catherine?" Shi Hua asked softly.

Mateqai let out a deep breath. "The errand I asked Nicholas to complete during our last long distance communication?"

She nodded. The two men seemed to be dancing around an issue, but it wasn't her place to ask. Her role was to facilitate their conversation.

"He sent a letter to her I'd written before we left Orrin."

"So you planned to stay in Jing the entire time?" Shi Hua tried not to let her surprise show.

"Forgive me, m'lady," he said. "I let my pride get in the way because I wanted you to ask me to stay. Chief Justice Anthea made me realize you were protecting the high brother by not saying anything to me. They both said it was my choice, not yours or theirs."

Pleasure and relief washed through Shi Hua. "Warden Matequi, would you do me the honor of becoming the captain of the empress's personal guard?"

"I am delighted to accept, Your Majesty." He executed a formal bow. When he straightened, he wore a pleased smile.

Shi Hua led the way down to the Huang He Balance gaol. Unlike the Issuran Temples tunneling into the bedrock, the Jing gaol walls in their larger cities were built by pouring concrete over steel rods in an earthen mold to form a basement. The construction was expensive but sturdier than wood, stone, or brick. In turn, the concrete and steel construction supported the larger pagodas built overtop the cells. Glass globes fueled with Light magic lit the area.

Anthea, Long Feather, and the Reverend Fathers were already present in the large center interrogation room. Chief Justice Li Chun sat on a stool. Her clerk sat on the chief justice's left, a portable desk on the younger woman's lap for her scroll and ink. Balance wardens lined the walls, their attention constantly moving from person to person. A Light priest sat to the chief justice's right.

Spell-threaded manacles chained the assassin to the floor. He was clean-shaven and of medium build. His hair hung loosely about his shoulders. Given that he was most probably a member of the Assassins Guild, the wardens hadn't given him a roughspun tunic. He sat cross-legged on the dirt floor. His hands rested on his knees in a meditation pose, and his eyes were closed.

Li Chun recited the date and time as well as the charges against the prisoner. "Brother Tianyu, please truthspell the prisoner."

Light magic enveloped the prisoner and tickled Shi Hua's skin. The prisoner's eyes opened and a horrible smile spread across his face. She felt the second Light spell activate.

"Anthea, freeze the room!"

Too late. She shielded her head with her arms as the massive explosion threw her into the concrete wall.

Chapter 19

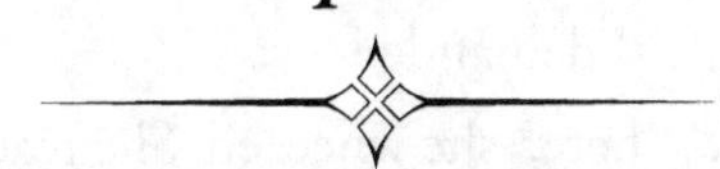

My ears rang, and a crushing weight lay on top of me. Did the explosion bring the entire Temple down on top of us? Did Luc get Po out of the building before Li Chun had the Light priest start his truth spell?

Shi Hua had shouted for me to freeze the room, but I hadn't been fast enough. The damn renegades had caught me with my leggings down once again, and I was mightily tired of always being behind in this race.

The weight on top of me shifted, and I groaned at the momentary pressure on my recently healed ribs.

"Balance help us," an unfamiliar voice said in Jing.

"Anthea! Anthea, answer me!" I knew Long Feather shouted in Issuran, but his voice was nearly drowned by the gong in my head.

"We are on a diplomatic mission, Warden." I couldn't tell if I whispered or shouted.

Something was in my eyes, and I scraped at the warm goo. When I dared to open them, I realized it was someone's flesh. I cursed as I flung it away.

Long Feather chuckled. "For an instant, we feared you had lost your face, m'lady."

Moans surrounded us, but I couldn't see much past the dust I breathed. I pulled a section of my hood over my nose and mouth. Long Feather help me to stand.

"I'm intact," I said. "Mateqai! Lady Shi Hua!"

"Here," she called out before she added, "Light, take me. Brother Tianyu is sorely injured."

From the bootsteps, Balance personnel raced down the stairs. Questions were asked and answered so fast in Jing, I had trouble keeping up with the various conversations.

"Where's Li Chun?" I demanded.

"I . . . am . . . still . . . here," she wheezed. She reached for something protruding from her chest.

"No, don't move the bone!" Chief Warden Junfeng ordered. "We need a healer in here. It's too close to her heart."

"Everyone, if you can walk, help someone who's slightly injured. Get upstairs and out of the way," a feminine voice commanded. "The healers are going to need room to treat those who cannot be moved."

"Where's the prisoner?" I asked.

"I think you're wearing part of him, Lady Justice," Long Feather muttered.

I looked down at my robes. Blood and viscera covered the front of me.

"Damn, I didn't even get to behead someone."

Li Chun's second, Justice Yi Nuo, got the injured out of the interrogation room and sealed the area. Her wardens checked on the other prisoners, but surprisingly, none of them were harmed. The concrete walls had contained the explosion.

I sat patiently outside the Temple as a healer checked me for injuries and her journeywoman took samples of the flesh and blood staining my robes.

The healer grimaced as she examined my eyes through a magnifying glass. "How does an Issuran healer check your eyes for injury?"

"Back home, both the Standora guild and the Orrin guild has extensive notes and drawings of how they look under normal circumstances." I smiled. "If the accused didn't have any blood-borne diseases, I should be fine."

"Healer?" The journeywoman held up a vial of something I couldn't see. Her senior took the vial and examined the contents through the glass.

"This needs to be tested to confirm," the healer ordered.

"What did you find?" Chief Warden Junfeng strode toward us followed by Luc and Yar.

"We think it's flash powder," the healer reported. "But we have to confirm it, Chief Warden."

Luc stared at me. "Are you all right?"

"Some bruises from where Long Feather and a local Balance warden dropped on me to protect me from the blast," I said wryly. "Otherwise, I'm fine."

"Really? Because you look like you've been swimming in offal."

I grinned. "That's good because I smell like it, too."

"Chief Warden Junfeng said the prisoner exploded?"

I nodded. "I think the renegades learned from the stunt we pulled with the langskips. The time-delay flashbangs using Light and Balance's magics?"

"A human can't possibly have a flash bang inside him," Junfeng protested.

"He could have swallowed many smaller clay balls," Luc suggested.

"Or a surgeon could have cut him open, implanted a spelled flashbang, and healed him," my healer said.

We all looked at her. Even her journeywoman seemed appalled and fascinated by the idea at the same time.

The healer shrugged as she packed her tools in her case. "You Temple people need to step up your game. Chief Justice, you out of all of us have seen the worst of humanity. Bend that view, and that will show what the demons are capable of." She stood and gestured for her journeywoman to follow her.

"You're not going to drag me to your guild house?" I asked as Junfeng helped me to my feet.

She paused and pivoted to face me. "Why? You're uninjured, and there are others who need my help." She turned back towards a group of warden with cuts and scrapes.

Luc frowned at me. "Where are Shi Hua, Mateqai, and Long Feather?"

"Our empress-to-be and her warden accompanied Brother Tianyu and Chief Justice Li Chun to the Healers House." I looked around us. "The last I saw my own warden, he was helping evacuate the Temple after he got me outside." I turned back to Luc. "The crown prince—"

"Already on his way to the duke's estate." Luc scowled. "We did find another assassin. A new cook with enough southern blue to take out the entire city."

"Still alive?" I asked.

He snickered. "I used a Light magic flashbang to disorient her, and she ran into the doorjamb and knocked herself out. Sister Xin Yan of Love pulled out her poison tooth. We were on our way here when we heard the explosion."

"High Brother?" Yar stared at the crowd of spectators outside the chest-high street level stone wall. Local peacekeepers held them in check, but it was more curiosity than violence that sparked the citizens.

"Yes?"

"The same Skoloti person is watching us."

One of the figures at the wall eased back into the crowd.

"The person in the hood with the odd pommel who just left," I asked.

"Yes." Yar turned to Junfeng. "Chief Warden?"

Unfortunately, Junfeng had the blank look of someone who was listening to silent speech. He shook himself. "You had a question, Warden Yar?"

"Are there any Skoloti who reside in Huang He?"

"Not that I know of." Junfeng frowned. "You might want to check with the Bureau of Residents to confirm this. Do you believe a Skoloti might be involved with the assassin we captured?"

"At this point, it would be pure speculation," Yar answered. "I only saw someone with Skoloti markings on their sword twice today. Both times involved our assassin. It was unusual enough to stand out to me."

"I can give you and the high brother directions to the Bureau of Residents if you wish to ask them," Junfeng said before he turned his attention to me. "Justice Yi Nuo would like to speak with you, m'lady. I told her about the flash powder and your experience with timed flashbangs."

Either she wanted my help in this investigation. Or I was about to be charged for being a renegade. Either way, my stomach rebelled, and I lost the delicious treats Li Chun's assistant had served me not so long ago.

Chapter 20

Another place. Another floor to pace.

Shi Hua tramped back and forth in the Healers House reception room. Mateqai and three Balance wardens who had been healed sat on the benches. Maybe she should have worn her boots instead of her brand new slippers. At the rate she paced today, the soles of this pair would wear out long before they reached Chengzhou.

A guild messenger raced through the room and out the door.

The elderly woman who attended the front desk returned and bowed to the Balance wardens. "I am sorry, but the master healer is still working with the chief justice."

She turned to Mateqai. "I grieve with you for the loss of your brother warden."

That meant the messenger was on his way to the Temple of Death before he informed the Huang He high brother of Light.

Mateqai nodded politely. "What about Brother Tianyu?"

"Like the chief justice, the healers are working with him." She gave Shi Hua a sad smile. "I am so sorry, Your Majesty. This should be a time of rejoicing for yours and the crown prince's nuptials. Would you care for some tea?"

"Your kindness honors me, but no thank you." Shi Hua matched the elderly woman's expression.

She inclined her head before she toddled over to her desk and continued with the embroidery she had been working on when the wagons transporting the most seriously injured from Balance arrived.

Two close calls in less than a day. Shi Hua couldn't tell if Thief was guarding her and her associates, or if He was taking potshots at them out of amusement. Either way, she'd needed something physical to release the stress. Unfortunately, running across rooftops was now out of the question.

The front door of the Healers manse opened to reveal Reverend Father Jin along with a squad of Light wardens. The priest's robes were splattered with blood and other bodily fluids, much like her own white silk mourning dress. No laundress would be able to eliminate those stains.

"Your Majesty." Reverend Father Jin bowed to her. "What is the status of the injured?"

Shi Hua relayed the same information she was given a moment before their arrival.

"High Brother Luc and his team have cleared the duke's manse of any potential problems," Reverend Father Jin reported. "Reverend Father Biming is escorting the crown prince to the ducal estate as we speak."

"And the Issuran portion of our party?" she asked.

"Warden Jonata and Mistress Yin Li are with the crown prince per your orders." His expression almost seemed to be one of pride. "High Brother Luc and Warden Yar are at the Temple of Balance, waiting on the healers to release Chief Justice Anthea and Warden Long Feather. Justice Yi Nuo has evacuated the Temple of Balance until the pagoda can be inspected for structural integrity."

"And the investigation into the incident?"

Reverend Father Jin gave a slight shake of his head. "Your Majesty, you are no longer Temple. This is Justice Yi Nuo's case as Chief Justice Li Chun's second. She knows her duty."

"But this is the second attack on a Balance Temple in Jing in as many months," Shi Hua pointed out.

"As both Justice Yi Nuo and High Brother Qianfan are aware." He gave her an odd look. "Do you have an objection to either them continuing the current investigation? You have that right as one of the victims, my lady."

Shi Hua sighed. "I have no objection to either person. I just wish—"

"Do you regret your decision?" He stared at her with an intensity that felt like disappointment.

Or maybe she was disappointed in herself. She had assumed she could keep Po safe and still continue doing her work with a bit of freedom. But her days of chasing renegades through the streets of Chengzhou, Kyoto, or Orrin were over.

She cleared her throat. "No, Reverend Father. It will take me some time to change old habits. I enjoyed my time in Orrin as a working priestess." She couldn't help her grin. "Maybe I enjoyed it a little too much."

Even he chuckled at her admission. "I had the same issue when I became a high brother and more so when I became Reverend Father. We are both doers at heart, but there comes a point when we must accept our roles as—leaders."

"Thank you for not calling me an elder." She knew her grin had turned impish.

"I would never be so uncouth as to mention a lady's age," he responded.

"Not when said lady could break one's nose," Mateqai said from behind her.

She glanced over her shoulder before she turned back to the Reverend Father. "And that's assuming my new captain of my personal guard doesn't challenge someone for such an insult besmirching my honor."

Reverend Father Jin frowned. "Does High Brother Luc know about this?"

"I have both his and Chief Justice Anthea's approval and blessing," Mateqai said. "And I'm sure they have forewarned Chief Warden Nicholas in Orrin."

Shi Hua shrugged. "Orrin's chief warden of Balance has been training a full regiment of wardens for the new Duchy of Anacapa. Nicholas will probably steal one or two of the recruits."

"And you are both stalling," the Reverend Father chided gently.

"Your Majesty?"

Shi Hua faced the Balance warden who spoke. "Yes?"

He bowed to her. "We would be happy to bring you word of the chief justice and the brother's condition once we know the results of the healings."

"Thank you, but I don't want to trouble you—"

The second Balance warden stood, and she also bowed. "Without your warning of the impending explosion, we would have had far more casualties. We owe you for the chance to save our chief justice."

Shi Hua inclined her head. "I pray the Twelve are watching over both Chief Justice Li Chun and Brother Tianyu, and they recover fully."

"Shall we, Your Majesty?" Reverend Father Jin indicated for her to precede him through the door.

Whatever initial suspicion she had, she quickly quelled. Two of his wardens took point. Once she cleared the doorway, Mateqai walked a half step behind and to her right. The Reverend Father paced her on her left. And the sadness that she could never go anywhere by herself ever again made her want to cry.

Now, she understood why Anthea chafed under the restrictions her Chief Warden Little Bear tried to place on her. Because if she didn't cry, she'd want to stab someone, too.

Chapter 21

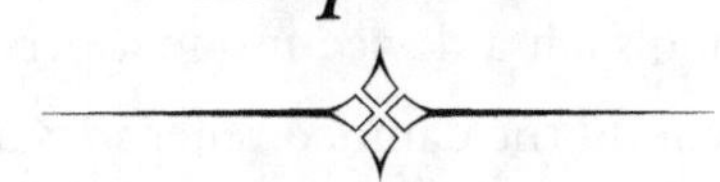

When we reached the bottom of the stairwell to the Balance gaol, Justice Yi Nuo and her warden stood facing the interrogation room. It appeared as if she examined the scene with her sightless eyes. Other than the broken glass globes being replaced by paper lanterns powered by Knowledge magic, the scene in the room was as we left it.

And the space reeked of death.

Justice Yi Nuo had pushed back her hood, displaying her straight hair pulled back in a neat queue at the base of her skull. She was nearly as tall as I was, with an angular face. Agitation flowed from her despite her calm exterior demeanor. That agitation explained her lack of etiquette by cutting to the chase instead of extending the usual niceties.

"I've sent the remaining accused to the Light and Peacekeeper gaols," she murmured. "The Temple of Balance will remain empty until the Imperial Architects Office can examine the structure. We may not have ground quakes on a regular basis like the Fire Islands, but we do have them. The building joints are designed to flex with the quakes, but there are no guarantees with a flash powder explosion of this magnitude."

I didn't know why she felt the need to explain things to me, other than she wanted someone higher ranked to reassure her. However, I felt so out of my depth I wasn't sure who needed reassurance more, her or me. So, I said nothing.

She continued, "Chief Warden Junfeng told me you used a time delay on flashbangs when you battled the skinwalkers while crossing the Peaceful Sea."

"Yes, Justice, we did," I said. "We also used Light magic to ignite the fuse instead of a torch."

"The chief warden also mentioned Healer Fen's theory of taking your idea and planting such a device inside a person." She sighed. "I guess I should be thankful the damned renegades didn't implant a demon egg inside our prisoner and use his death to hatch it."

"I have tried very hard not to think of that possibility, Justice," I said. "I still have nightmares about people I personally knew who were used to hatch demon eggs."

"But you and I have to think about those possibilities in order to prevent them from happening again." There was no bite in Yi Nuo's words. Only a terrible, aching sadness. "I was in Chengzhou two months ago when the attack happened."

That tidbit caught me by surprise. "May I ask why?"

"Our Reverend Mother had rotating classes for all the justices in Jing. We practiced some of the techniques you developed from your battles with the enemy," she said.

"I hope you realize those were not true tactics. I was pulling half-crazed ideas from my buttocks in desperation," I replied.

For the first time, her manner eased, and she chuckled. "I think the Reverend Mother was hoping to inspire us to think on our feet as you do. If we don't know what we are doing, how can our opponents anticipate our actions?" She quickly sobered. "However, all I felt today was unadulterated terror, and I wasn't even down here. How did Lady Shi Hua know there was a problem?"

"She was a Light priestess of unusual sensitivity," Luc said. "She detected the internal spell on the prisoner the instant it activated."

"Unfortunately, neither Chief Justice Li Chun nor I were fast enough to freeze the room," I grumbled.

"The union between Lady Shi Hua and the crown prince makes much more sense." Yi Nuo nodded. "The nobility can be idiots in their demands, but if a former Light priestess can bear Light talented imperial heirs, it will relieve the nobles' misgivings about the new emperor."

"I know part of their problem is Empress Bao Yu having a child with a commoner, but what is the issue with Quan having a slight touch of Thief talent?" I asked.

"I don't like correcting a senior justice, but for your sake and the crown prince's, do not refer to his father's family name," she gently chided.

"My apologies," I murmured. "I meant no disrespect."

"I know." She sighed. "The nobles don't trust the Temple of Thief. Mainly because several have had their necks on the wrong end of a justice's blade, thanks to accusations of treason."

I stared at her. "Thief would only have them arrested if they were demon dealing."

"If Thief follows their code in Issura, then your citizens are quite fortunate."

Whatever was really happening in Jing, I needed to know. I quickly warded the room. "Yi Nuo, please tell me what happened. I swore to Queen Teodora I would get the crown prince home safely. If there's something happening here that affects the crown prince's security, I need to know." I waited several heartbeats for her to say something. Anything.

"There have been cases over the past century were Thief has accused certain nobles of wrongdoing," she said. "Alleged portable assets have disappeared between the arrests and the inventory by the local Bureaus of Weights and Measures. Plus, Thief has purchased the real estate at auction when there were no other bidders."

"No other bidders?" Luc exclaimed.

"We've learned of rumors that any other merchant or noble who wished to purchase were—encouraged not to bid," she said. "However, Balance's attempts to trace the truth have been futile."

"You would have cause to truthspell them if you believe there has been blackmail, extortion, or fraud," I blurted.

"Only one merchant in Chengzhou agreed to a truthspell." She shook her head. "He met a most unfortunate accident. After that, none of them would speak with anyone from Balance."

"And you cannot truthspell anyone without their permission when they have not been charged with a crime." Such an obvious result. Our own ethics were being used against us.

"An unfortunate accident?" Luc prompted.

"He tumbled over the balcony railing from his third story study and broke his neck," Yi Nuo's warden volunteered. "The city peacekeepers found paraphernalia for smoking soma in his office, but everyone who knew him said he had no vices."

"What did the time rewind spell show?" I asked.

"There was a trap spell," Yi Nuo said bitterly. "Justice Caihong was killed. Justice Mei Wen took over the case. As she described it to me, when she tried the rewind, it was as if time had been erased."

Shock ran through me. This couldn't be a mere coincidence. "Justice Mei Wen? Is there more than one justice by that name in Jing?"

"No." Yi Nuo scowled. "Do you know her?"

"We've never met in person," I said. "We've spoken a few times through distance speech. I felt her pain when she was injured during the demon attack on the palace and Temples in Chengzhou. Your information casts a different light on the situation."

Yi Nuo was no fool. I could tell she was searching her recollections of that night. She reached for her warden's hand. He gripped hers tightly and closed his eyes.

"I thought I was imagining it," she whispered.

"Imagining what?" I demanded.

She relaxed, and her warden opened his eyes.

"The demons were focused on particular justices during their attack." Yi Nuo cocked her head. "I don't mean to ask an intrusive personal question, Chief Justice, but why were you distance speaking with Mei Wen prior to your assignment as Issura's ambassador?"

I glanced at Luc, and he nodded. However, I wasn't sure how much I wanted to reveal. It wasn't suspicion of the Huang He justice, but a fear I would put Yi Nuo in danger if she knew too much.

"Justice Mei Wen has been good friends with Lady Shi Hua since their novice years," I said. "After our initial introduction, we've been exchanging information on our rulers' behalf."

Yi Nuo digested that bit of knowledge. She was smart enough not to ask further questions. "I don't like this," she muttered under her breath. "I don't like this one bit. May I ask one more favor of you, Chief Justice?"

"If I can," I said.

"Would you and High Brother Luc assist us in the rewind for the interrogation room? I don't want to miss any pertinent detail."

"Are you sure you want foreign clergy involved?" Luc asked.

Yi Nuo nodded sharply. "Right now, I trust you more than our own Reverend Mothers and Fathers."

My heart ached in sympathy for the woman. She found herself in the same damned position I often found myself—very little trust, a mass of questions, and enemies targeting me and those who were close to me.

Chapter 22

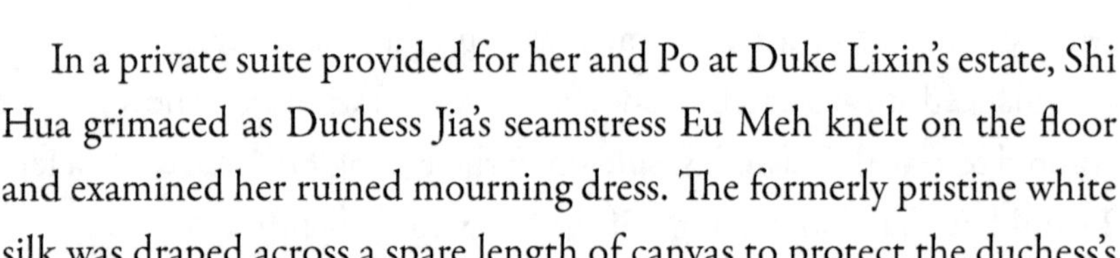

In a private suite provided for her and Po at Duke Lixin's estate, Shi Hua grimaced as Duchess Jia's seamstress Eu Meh knelt on the floor and examined her ruined mourning dress. The formerly pristine white silk was draped across a spare length of canvas to protect the duchess's rugs. The older woman clucked and shook her head.

"There is no way I can clean this, Your Majesty." She looked up at Shi Hua and Jia. "I could sew a new dress for you, but it would take a few days."

"Thank you for your honest assessment, Eu Meh." Shi Hua smiled. "I suspected as much."

The seamstress held up the garment and cocked her head. "What I could do is clean your dress and dye it if you would like. It would be a shame to destroy a beautiful brand new outfit."

"It's covered in blood!" Duchess Jia protested with an appalled expression.

"That's slightly better than the face full of the renegade's liver like Chief Justice Anthea or one of his ribs through my chest like Chief Justice Li Chun," Shi Hua quipped.

Neither the duchess nor her seamstress looked amused. In fact, both of them looked appalled and a little sick to their stomachs. Shi Hua bit her lower lip. Maybe Po was right. She had picked up a few bad habits from Anthea.

"We thank the Twelve you were not injured or killed, Your Majesty," Mateqai chided gently. "Our apologies, Your Grace, Mistress Eu Meh. Her Majesty's black sense of humor is her way of dealing with attempts on her life."

"I do not believe I was the target, Captain," she shot back.

"I beg your pardon, Your Majesty, anyone with Balance and Light talents were targets by that renegade." Mateqai frowned at her. "That includes you."

"Maybe I'm finally not thinking of myself as Temple." She shot him a nasty look. Mateqai rolled his eyes.

On the way to the duke's estate, she made the Reverend Father and his party stop at a second-hand shop. Inside, she found decent accoutrements for a mercenary, including boots to fit him. That was better than him wearing his warden uniform. Fewer questions would be asked.

She also helped him comb and secure his hair in a proper warrior's topknot. She'd never suggest he cut his hair. Issurans of Chumash decent like Mateqai only cut their hair when in mourning.

Unfortunately, that left his sword and knives. The ornaments on the pommels displayed the symbol for the Temple of Light. However, the merchant had spare strips of leather, when tied in place hid the damning symbols. Shi Hua promised she would have new weapons forged for both of them once they reached Chengzhou.

"You two sound like quarreling lovers," the duchess commented.

Shi Hua stared at her in horror.

"With all due respect, Your Grace, that is how ugly rumors start and wind up getting people killed," Mateqai said coolly.

Eu Meh ducked her head, but she couldn't stop tittering at her employer being called on her gossip.

"How dare you speak to me that way!" Duchess Jia snapped at him. "You are a commoner!"

"He has a point," Shi Hua said. "I am as much a Bao as you are, Your Grace. Is this the way in which you wish to start our familial relationship?"

"I-I—" Her attention darted about the room, seeking an escape. "I meant nothing by it, Your Majesty."

"Then maybe you should apologize to the empress before her husband and yours hears of this, Your Grace," Eu Meh prompted.

"I apologize for my ill-considered words, Your Majesty," the duchess said softly with a bow.

"Your apology is accepted, Your Grace." Shi Hua turned to Eu Meh. "How long would it take for you to clean and dye the dress?"

The seamstress looked at the ceiling as she calculated the time needed. "It would be best to take apart your dress for an even color. Five to six days, Your Majesty."

"We won't be in Huang He for that long." Shi Hua shook her head. "That's one thing both Captain Huizhong and Captain Mateqai agree upon. Can you wash out the worst of the dirt and blood before bundling the dress so my other clothes are not ruined? I'm sure we can find someone at the palace who can dye it for me."

"As you wish, Your Majesty." Eu Meh bowed and gathered the garment and canvas before she trundled off on her errand.

"I pray you and the emperor are not leaving early because of my thoughtlessness, Your Majesty," Duchess Jia murmured.

"No, it's most definitely not that." Shi Hua took the other woman's beringed hand into both of hers. "My husband fears putting you and your family in danger by staying here. He cares a great deal for your husband. Other than his mother, his brother, and his nephews, Lixin is the one other family member he speaks most affectionately of."

"I hired the cook who was arrested." Tears glistened in the duchess's eyes. "Her credentials were impeccable. I even hired a messenger falcon to confirm she had actually been employed at Duchess Lan Ying's estate."

"You did everything correctly, Jia," Shi Hua said firmly. "There's no need for self-recrimination. The renegades find ways to get past our defenses, mainly by telling the truth. As my husband has said many times, they are playing a long game that if they win, they will still lose. The demons will keep their human allies alive as long as they useful."

"The cook would have murdered my children to get at the emperor, wouldn't she?"

"Yes," Shi Hua said. "The only reason Chief Justice Elizabeth of Tandor in Issura survived the poisoning of her entire Temple was she hated goat stew."

Despite her threatening tears, Jia giggled. "I'm glad to know I'm not the only one who detests goat."

"As I'm sure High Brother Luc or one of the Light priests assisting him has already told you, any potential hires should be truthspelled before they are employed." Shi Hua gently squeezed the other woman's hand. "And ask your own high brother to perform random checks with your staff. I don't want anything to happen to you, Duke Lixin, or any of your children."

"Thank you for your kindness, Your Majesty." After Shi Hua released her, Jia executed a perfect bow and left the sitting room of the suite.

"You need to watch your back with that one," Mateqai murmured.

"I agree with the warden." Reverend Father Biming stepped into the sitting room from the balcony.

"Now you're resorting to spying on me?" Shi Hua said dryly.

"I came to make sure you were all right." Cuts marred his left cheek and his forehead. "You took off with Brother Tianyu without thinking."

"My new dress was the only casualty," she said lightly.

"This is not a laughing matter, young lady." He scowled at her. For the first time, she truly noticed the lines in his face. Worry and age fought over who would scar him next.

"Neither is spying on the empress," Mateqai said fiercely. "Either you trust her or you don't. At least, be honest with her on which way you lean."

"Mind your place, Warden," Biming snapped.

Mateqai's eyes narrowed. "That's captain to you, Reverend Father."

His statement took Biming aback. "What?"

"Mateqai is now the captain of the empress's guard," Shi Hua said coldly. "You do not have a say in this matter. I thought we had settled things between us when we left Naha. As my captain asked, do you trust me or not?"

Biming shook his head. "I don't know if I even know you anymore."

"I'm exactly what you trained me to be." Fury rose unbidden within her. "Bao Quan Po's shadow, to protect him against all enemies foreign and domestic. Have you changed your mind about recruiting me? Or will I find myself dead while you find a more biddable empress?"

"I—" A sad expression fell over his visage. "I have overstepped, Your Majesty. I beg for your forgiveness."

She doubted if he'd ever begged for anything in his life. Stolen or cajoled maybe, but never begged.

"Between this morning's assassination attempt on Po, finding a renegade within the duke's staff, and the explosion during the accused's interrogation, we are all on edge, Reverend Father." She put on a wan smile. "Perhaps it's best if we all get a good night's sleep. Then if you have reasonable objections to my choice as captain of my guard, I'll entertain your logic."

"Yes, Your Majesty." Biming bowed.

"And Reverend Father?"

He straightened. "Yes?"

"From now on, please use the appropriate door." She gestured at Mateqai. "Captain, please escort the Reverend Father out."

The Issuran's expression remained stolid, but she felt a thread of pleasure from him. It was akin to the same emotion he'd felt when Anthea castigated a drunk Luc for harassing Shi Hua when she was pregnant.

Yes, she'd definitely made a good choice by hiring Mateqai to head her security detail. She just prayed he wouldn't regret it years down the road.

Chapter 23

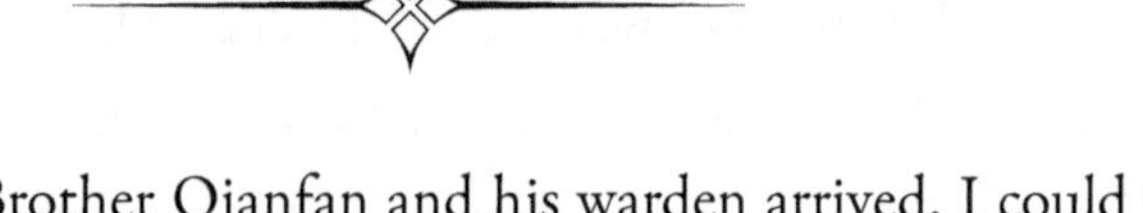

When High Brother Qianfan and his warden arrived, I could feel the grief emanating from the Huang He seat. He pushed back his hood and approached Luc.

"The Empress and the warden you assigned to her rendered aid to my injured people, and they stayed at the Healers Guild until Reverend Father Jin insisted she go to a more secure facility."

I tensed at Qianfan's words. People often did out of character things when they were this upset. I prayed to Balance he didn't blame Shi Hua for anyone's death.

"Please tell them thank you for their kindness," he added.

I sagged in relief. Maybe I was too used to being blamed when things went wrong. Or maybe I blamed myself. I hadn't frozen this room in time to save anyone.

"W-who—" Yi Nuo choked on the word.

"Warden Sile," Qianfan replied. "Brother Tianyu will survive. The majority of the damage was to his vocal cords. The chief justice's outlook is not as assured. They healed the damage to her left lung, but her heart seized while they worked. The chief healer will not know her absolute prognosis until she awakes."

He crossed to Yi Nuo and embraced her. "If you are not up to a rewind, ask one of the other justices to assist Chief Justice Anthea."

"No." She sniffed as Qianfan released her. "No," she repeated more strongly. "I refuse to cower in the face of the renegades' perverted tactics."

"What about Chunhua?" he asked her. "Tianyu asked about her safety."

"All the babies and the Justice women expecting are at Mother," she answered.

Of course, we weren't the only nation dealing with the edict to birth as many children with Light talent as we could. And if Yi Nuo had a child with Tianyu, it would explain why she was on edge. Part of the renegades' plan could very well have been to bring down the Temple itself and kill everyone within.

Including the children.

Qianfan turned to me. "Chief Justice, Chief Warden Junfeng reported your conversation with Healer Fen to me. If the demons use their phasing ability to implant their eggs within a human, couldn't they also to the same with a flashbang?"

"Yes, they could." I held up a hand to stall his next question. "Before we continue, High Brother, would you mind if we set aside titles while we work on this investigation?"

He chuckled. "You have adopted Li Chun's rules?"

"Actually, we have the same policy in Orrin as you do in Huang He." I smiled. "However, Li Chun is correct that such a policy saves a great deal of time and saliva."

"Do you mind if our wardens stay down here, Anthea?" Yi Nuo asked.

"She's been training her wardens and mine to witness rewinds," Luc said.

"Well, at the rate I was losing Light priests over the last year, I needed to do something to keep up with our caseload," I replied.

Long Feather laughed.

"She's also recruited members of the other eleven Temples," Yar added.

"High Mother Leocadia volunteered," I protested.

Qianfan grunted. "Yours is not the only nation with that problem. Thankfully, our Reverend Father understands if he wants to keep the ports open, he needs to supply us with enough personnel."

"Our issue is being stuck in tradition," Luc grumbled. "The rules regarding the admission of women to Light need to be changed."

Qianfan scowled. "Let me guess. They won't allow men in the Temple of Love either?"

"Closest Issura will come is admitting *berda*," I said. Love wouldn't even allow a *berda* to be High Sister until I pushed the issue.

"We have too many people in Jing and too much work to be that picky about who we can exclude," Yi Nuo said softly. "But we need to focus on our immediate problem. Discover what exactly happened here and devise a way to prevent it from happening again."

I blew out a deep breath. "I've never worked with concrete before. Do you have any recommendations?"

"It would be easier to show you." She grimaced. "If we can find places to sit without soaking our uniforms in blood."

"Here." I unbuckled my sword harness and handed it to Long Feather. "My robes have dried while I was sitting in the sun. Sit on them so you don't ruin your own." I untied the lacings and stripped off the garment before I handed it to Yi Nuo's warden. He led her to a relatively bare spot on the dirt floor and spread out my robes for her to sit upon.

I found another clean spot opposite of her.

And realized it was clear was because I'd caught the blood and viscera on my face and cloak. I hoped I would have a chance to bathe before I retired for the evening. Despite Healer Fen's efforts to clean my skin to make sure none of the blood was mine, my hairline was a bit crusty.

I sat cross-legged on the comparably clean dirt, rested one palm on the walls and the other on the ground, and extended my senses toward Yi Nuo. She had a marvelously ordered mind. Since Haung He was a port city like Orrin, she generally handled the inn brawls, petty theft, and the occasional smuggling. And she thanked Balance for sparing her and her daughter during the demon attacks in Chengzhou.

Yi Nuo pulled me into her understanding of the components of the surrounding walls. The parts sang like a choir. Individual grains of sand chimed sweet soprano, pieces of gravel belted the melody, and iron bars tolled the bass notes. The earth thrummed with its own heartbeat.

"Everyone in position to observe?" Yi Nuo asked.

The Light priests and wardens murmured their compliance. She and I chanted the rewind spell. We were only going back a few hours, but the strings of time didn't want to cooperate.

Hold a moment, I silently told her. *I've had a trap spell placed in the past that traveled with the rewind. It almost killed me.*

She clenched her muscles to keep hold of the various lines while I carefully felt along them.

There. Do you detect it?

That's a particularly wicked piece of work. Yi Nuo examined the spell. *How do we dissipate it without killing everyone in the room?*

This magic was attached to the assassin. Not attached. Entangled with his spirit in the past.

Shi Hua? Are you busy? I called.

I'm being tortured by Duchess Jia's maids in preparation for attending dinner. No wonder she felt perturbed. She enjoyed state functions as much as I did. *What do you need, and who's with you?*

Justice Yi Nuo and I are trying to perform the rewind in the Balance interrogation room. There's a trap spell on the assassin that's designed to activate the moment we pull the past into the present.

Shi Hua's alarm shot through me, and heated water sloshed against her skin. *Let it go! It's not worth your lives!*

Calm down, I retorted. *We're not that idiotic. It's woven through the assassin's spirit on purpose, but it feels like your description of what Yanaba accidentally did to herself when the demons invaded my Temple last year, and she clung to Mya's tracking magic while activating the Balance last resort spells. Can you show me how you and Jeremy unraveled her?*

That was more like a tangled skein of yarn after a cat played with it. Shi Hua showed me how they saved Yanaba. *You must be slow and patient. You rush, and the assassin will drag you into Death's arms with him.*

Shi Hua withdrew partially from me and relayed the problem to Luc and Qianfan.

All we need to do is undo the seal of the spell, Yi Nuo said. *The unraveling should be fairly simple.*

That's what worries me, I grumbled.

Together we carefully plucked at the seal or rather the knot. I held strands out of the way while Yi Nua carefully unwound the end. I tried to ignore the cold sweat dripping down my body and the trembling of my limbs.

Shall I? she asked when the knot was untangled.

We're both going to die no matter which us makes a mistake unbinding this spell.

On three, she whispered. *One, two, three.* She gently pulled on the end of the spell.

It unraveled with so much force I couldn't keep my grip on the timeline. The present snapped into place, and I sagged against the concrete wall.

Somehow, everyone in the room was still alive.

"Anthea?" Luc shuffled toward me, but Long Feather beat him to my position. My warden unslung the water skin over his shoulder and helped me take a few sips.

I patted his arm. "You and Jonata are both getting additional bonuses for going above and beyond."

"I'll hold you to that." He grinned. "And I have High Brother Luc as a witness."

Across the room, Yi Nuo's warden and Qianfan assisted her.

In the back of my mind, Shi Hua laughed bitterly. *Now, we know where the extra power of the explosion came from.*

Guilt assaulted me. A warden had paid the ultimate price because I didn't keep control of the timeline.

"It wasn't your fault. Not when it already happened, Anthea," Yi Nuo said.

"Let me know when you're ready to do this rewind," I growled. "I want as much information as we can get before we interrogate the female Luc caught at the duke's manse."

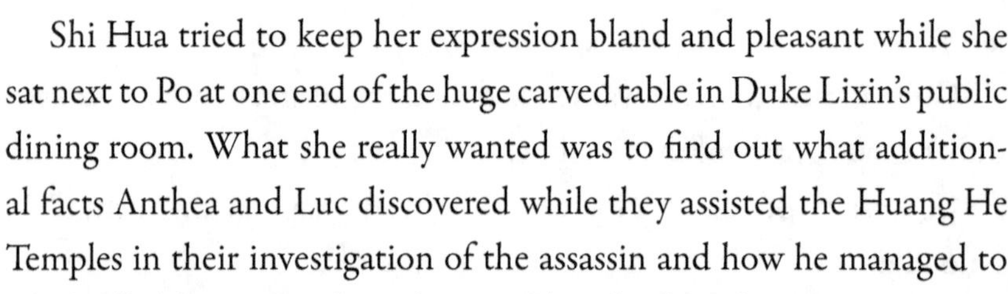# Chapter 24

Shi Hua tried to keep her expression bland and pleasant while she sat next to Po at one end of the huge carved table in Duke Lixin's public dining room. What she really wanted was to find out what additional facts Anthea and Luc discovered while they assisted the Huang He Temples in their investigation of the assassin and how he managed to get the flashbang into the Balance gaol in the first place.

Anthea dressed in her formal black chiton and sandals while Luc wore the Issuran Light dress uniform of a deerskin vest and leggings decorated with porcupine quills, pearls, and gold beads. They made a striking couple, and there was a certain regal air about them Shi Hua could marginally imitate.

The Reverend Fathers also attended the dinner. Jin seemed preoccupied, possibly because of High Brother Qianfan's report on the explosion inside the Temple of Balance. Biming seemed determined to be gracious and charming despite the two confrontations he and Shi Hua had over the past few days. Or maybe because of those disagreements.

The last thing she wanted was to make an enemy of him. He was exceptionally clever and could be extremely dangerous. Of that she had no doubt. However, he needed to realize they were now equals, whether he agreed to her new status or not.

None of the wardens were present. Only Mateqai and Huizhong

were permitted in the room as the captains of the Imperial Guard. They stood at attention behind her and Po.

She hated not knowing what happened after Anthea and Yi Nuo disabled the trap spell tied to the assassin's spirit. However, Duchess Jia would consider such a topic at her dinner table uncouth.

And Po needed his cousin Duke Lixin's support.

"What is your opinion of Duke Bao Mengchang as grand chancellor?" Po asked.

"He has the same high opinion of himself he had when we were children." Lixin smiled. "But your brother had no complaints concerning his service that I know of. The one thing he did correctly was to recommend the emperor execute Wu Sunshu."

A chill ran through Shi Hua at the mention of Emperor Chengwu's father.

Po paused and lowered his eating sticks. "And your thought on the fate of Wu Sunshu?"

Lixin sighed and shook his head. "I attended the trials. There is no question he committed treason."

"It has been a difficult day, my husband," Duchess Jia interjected. "This talk of violence upsets my digestion."

What in the Twelve would this woman do when faced with a demon attack? Throw her manners at the invaders? Shi Hua plucked a piece of bok choy and chewed it to keep from saying her thoughts aloud.

"My apologies, my wife." Lixin favored Jia with an affectionate smile.

Po paid down his eating sticks and leaned back in his chair. "While I have no wish to upset your digestion, Your Grace, I would have my cousin speak frankly because I trust his counsel."

Biming's reaction to Po's words was so slight Shi Hua wouldn't have noticed without her training outside of Light. Did Biming expect to be Po's primary counselor at court? The Temples' traditionally didn't interfere in civilian rule unless the leader of a nation took steps that would potentially harm the human race.

Jia glanced at Shi Hua who continued to nibble her dinner silently. The duchess's cheeks flushed. Maybe she realized the future empress was displaying more decorum than she was. Or maybe she realized Po's rebuke for what it was—that she shouldn't undermine her husband in front of the emperor.

"I apologize for speaking out of turn, Your Majesty." Jia inclined her head. "Of course, I am glad you believe my husband is looking out for the empire's best interest."

"The crown prince's aid to Issura has been invaluable." Anthea saluted Po with her cup of tea. "I'm sure your husband's aid to him will be equally invaluable."

"You don't want to lose any trade deals," Po responded. "Particularly, the import of Jing tea."

"I admit I have selfish reasons for continuing our nations' friendship." Anthea smiled. "And you know my staff in Orrin would heartily agree."

Everyone at the table laughed.

"If Crown Princess Chiara weren't already married, I'm sure Queen Teodora would have negotiated a marriage contract between our nations," Po added. "As it is, I'm glad I avoided such matters until now. I wouldn't have such a lovely wife." He took Shi Hua's hand and gently squeezed.

She smiled back. They needed to present a united front, and with Jia's penchant for gossip, this was a good place to start.

"As the chief justice would say, balance in all things," Shi Hua replied.

"To answer your original concern, Your Majesty, Mengchang has done his best to hold things until your return to Jing," Lixin said. "But he doesn't have as strong as a claim to the throne as Prince Bao Pu,

Duke Bao Guang, Duke Bao Xi, or I do. Frankly, I have no wish for the Dragon Throne, and I sympathize for the trials you'll face in Chengzhou after the attempts on your life earlier today."

"You simply don't want to be a target," Po teased.

"No, I don't," Lixin responded. "As High Brother Luc pointed out to me, simply bearing the name Bao makes me and my family vulnerable to the renegades. You are the last surviving son of Empress Bao Yu, and we need to unite behind you to survive whatever comes next."

Po and Lixin continued to talk through the rest of the meal with occasional comments and questions from the Reverend Fathers. Anthea and Luc remained silent when it came to Jing internal politics, but Shi Hua knew they were paying close attention to what was unsaid as much as what was.

She was relieved when Jia asked about foods and clothing styles in Issura. As much as she disliked frivolous topics, her own stomach churned with anxiety over what faced them at the Imperial Palace.

Chapter 25

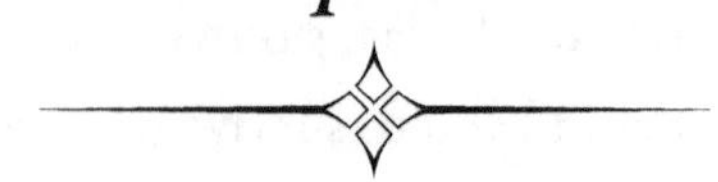

The wardens and guards had added a bed to Po and Shi Hua's room for Yin Li and her son by the time we returned to the massive suite after dinner. They'd also set up pallets for themselves in the sitting room.

My own stomach issues came back with a vengeance despite the wonderful dinner the duke and duchess's staff had served. Bird's nest soup sounded odd, but it was delicious, and I didn't want the cooks' efforts to go to waste.

"Does anyone still have some of Healer Bly's stomach elixir?" I asked.

"No, Chief Justice," Guardsman Zhao answered. "But I did pick up a similar potion in the Huang He market this afternoon." He retrieved the bottle from his pack and handed it to me.

"Why did you purchase nausea medicine today?" Captain Huizhong frowned.

"I had him do it," Po interjected. "In case—" He stared at the ceiling as he realized everyone in the room stared at him.

"You impregnated your wife before we reach Chengzhou, and she is tortured with morning sickness?" I prompted.

"I've also noticed you have been taking an inordinate amount of the medication," Po shot back. "Is there something you wish to share with everyone, Chief Justice?"

"If I were pregnant, I would be showing by now," I growled.

"Not necessarily," Yin Li said. "I didn't begin to show until—" She quickly quieted at my glare.

"Not that it's anyone's business, but I am not pregnant, I can never be pregnant, and my problems are a side effect of the Assassins Guild poisoning the Healers Guild's oil supply over a year ago."

Luc stepped to my side. "You didn't tell me—"

"I'm sorry. I didn't want you to worry over nothing either of us have any control over." I released a deep breath. "Both Sivan and Master Bly have been listening for my health."

"Has she consulted with Masters Aaron and Devin?" Luc asked.

"This is exactly why she didn't tell you, High Brother," Shi Hua snapped before she turned to face her husband. "And Anthea will know I am with child before either of us, so stop jumping to congratulate your penis."

We all stared at her. The outburst was so unlike the young woman.

She seemed to crumple. "I'm sorry, Po. I thought I could be the wife you needed me to be. But I don't know if I can keep up this act."

"Shi Hua—" He started forward.

"Come, my lady." I wrapped my arm about the smaller woman's shaking shoulders. "Come into my bedchamber and compose yourself."

As I guided her to mine and Luc's room, Yin Li whispered to her son. The boy immediately went to Yar's side. The Love priestess followed us into the room and closed the door. Yin Li warded the chamber while I guided Shi Hua to the side of the bed and settled her. The Love priestess sat on the other side of her niece.

"Is this about Biming?" Yin Li murmured.

"That's only part of it." Shi Hua swiped at her lids to keep her tears from falling, but she smeared the coal the maid had applied around her eyes.

I rose and crossed the room to my bag. After retrieving a handkerchief from one of the side pockets, I handed it to the future empress. She wiped her face.

"Zhao told me," Yin Li said. "You were in the right. I'm proud of you for standing up for yourself."

A distraught Shi Hua meant Biming had done something idiotic. The knowledge and stress didn't help my stomach issues. After a quick swig of the potion, I recorked the bottle, set it aside, and pulled out my dagger.

"Which room is his?" I growled.

"Anthea!" Yin Li gasped. "That's sacrilege!"

"What did the demon-assed, insensitive charlatan do?" I demanded.

Shi Hua related her confrontation with Biming aboard the *Unbridled* after we left Naha Harbor. The pair had a second argument when he snuck into our suite this afternoon.

"I was already nervous about our arrival in Jing." She gulped past the tears rolling down her cheeks. "But it's been one thing after another, and normally, I could focus on the task at hand, but now I can't do anything for myself as empress, and I don't know how to deal with feeling helpless. I've never felt helpless before. I thought I could handle this new role, but it's nothing like I've—I've—I—" She gasped for air like she couldn't breathe.

I understood the helpless feeling. All I could do was watch while Yin Li rubbed the middle of Shi Hua's back and whispered calming words in her niece's ear.

"Yin Li, could you please lower your wards?" I said.

"I can, but I'd feel better if you left your dagger here." She shot me a wry smile. Shi Hua even managed a weak giggle. I kept forgetting how young she was. How much had rested on her shoulders for nearly a decade. As High Sister Mya told me, everyone had a breaking point.

"Can we agree that I sheathe it?"

Yin Li nodded. The feather brush of Love magic faded.

I frowned as I put away my weapon. "Aren't you going to try to talk me out of what I'm about to do?"

Yin Li scowled over the top of her niece's head. "It needs to be done, and he might actually respect you. He's in the suite one door down from ours."

I stalked out of the room and closed the door behind me. Love magic caressed my skin again. Yin Li could do a better job than me at comforting the troubled Shi Hua. But there were some things I could handle.

The men in the sitting room, even Luc, stared at me. I ignored them and marched for the main entry.

"Chief Justice?" Jonata said.

"What?" I snapped and whirled to face her.

She lifted her chin. "Can you get your lightning under control before you blast the duke's manse apart? Huang He already has one building of questionable stability." Her gaze dropped to my hands.

I looked down. Sparks arched between my fingers.

I returned my attention to Jonata and gave her a smile I'm sure wasn't very nice. "I won't quench my power just yet, Warden, but I promise not to destroy our host's home."

She nodded. "Thank you, Chief Justice."

I stalked out of our suite and down the hall. When I knocked on the next door, I left scorch marks on the lacquer. I gritted my teeth. More gold out of my pocket for recompense.

Brother Fa opened the door. The huge man raised an eyebrow at the lateness of the evening before his attention dropped to my hands.

I narrowed my eyes. "I will speak with Reverend Father Biming."

He nodded and stepped aside for me to enter. Brother Jian and the wardens had set up pallets much like the guards in the suite I shared with the royal couple. Jian rose, an angry look on his face. My expression probably matched his.

Of course, he had felt Shi Hua's distress. She'd mentioned they were fast friends when they were novices.

Jian marched to the bedchamber on the left and banged on the door. "Reverend Father Biming!"

Reverend Father Jin poked his head out of the other bedchamber. His hair fell about his shoulders and he wore a silk dressing robe. "What the demon is going on out here?"

Biming's door opened. Like Jin, his hair was in disarray, but he only wore silk pants. "That's what I'd like to know."

"Coming after me is one thing," I bit out. "Sabotaging your own empress is another. Do you have any idea what that girl has been through for the last eight years?"

Biming opened his mouth, but I poked him in the chest. He jerked at the mild shock I gave him.

"You don't know because you don't care about her. She's just a tool to you." I jabbed my left forefinger in the direction of the royal suite. A forefinger that emitted jagged little bolts of lightning.

"She has done everything you have asked of her. She's protected your precious Po, even from himself at times. Yet, you've been doing everything you can to undermine her since we arrived in Naha."

"Whatever Warden Mateqai said—"

"Mateqai?" Why the hell was Biming trying to distract me? "First of all, he hasn't said a damn thing to me since we stepped onto Jing soil. Second of all, he's no longer a warden."

I stepped closer to Biming, and he took two steps back to stay out of my reach. It wasn't lost on me that not even the Thief wardens moved to interfere.

"I'm talking about Shi Hua," I continued. "If you took issue with her marrying Po, you should have said something weeks ago." A horrible thought suddenly occurred to me, and I stepped away from him. "But that's assuming you're really Biming."

"What?" An incredulous expression filled his visage. "How dare you—"

"Jin—" I started, but the Reverend Father of Light was already casting the truthspell. The hiss of blades sliding from scabbards filled the room.

Biming's mouth hung open as the Light magic settled around him.

"What is your real name?" I demanded.

His shoulders sagged. "My birth name was Xiyang. Biming was the name of my great-grandfather who died in the last invasion. I choose it as my religious name to honor him."

"Why did you assume I was demon-influenced when I returned to Naha?"

Fury exploded from him. "I don't believe you because I've never met anyone who escaped from them."

"I admitted I had help," I snapped.

"Of course, two of the Twelve appeared to personally help you," he sneered.

"It happened to me once before. During the Battle of Tandor." I shook my head sadly. "Don't you believe in the Twelve?"

Once again, his mouth fell open until the truthspell prodded him to answer my question.

"No."

Tension filled the room.

"So, you didn't believe Shi Hua when she reported her experience with Balance?"

"No," he choked out.

A terrible lump developed in my throat. Despite my own doubts, I had discovered my faith existed after my experiences. The Twelve answered me when I truly needed their guidance, but they trusted me to find my own answers rather than me relying on them like a child depending on their parents.

I swallowed hard. "Why do you even want to be Reverend Father of Thief if you don't believe in Him?"

"Because I have nothing else." He watched me with pleading eyes. "Please stop this, Anthea."

The sadness in his voice made my heart ache. "I just have two more questions. Are you part of the renegade movement?"

"No."

"Are you a demon?"

"No."

I turned to Reverend Father Jin and nodded. The tingle of Light magic disappeared.

"Regardless of your personal feelings about our deities, the emperor and empress need your support, Biming. If there is any love in your heart left for Po, please help him and his wife." Not expecting an answer, I turned and left their sitting room.

I was halfway down the hall when Brother Jian called out, "Chief Justice?"

I pivoted to face him. "Yes?"

"Is she—is Lady Shi Hua all right?" Concern rolled off him and filled the corridor.

"She will be." I glanced over my shoulder at the door to our suite. "It's been a taxing two months for all of us, but today was particularly stressful with an assassination this morning and a state dinner tonight."

"Is there anything I can do to help her?" he whispered.

"Do what you and Fa have always done." I smiled at him. "Be her friend. That's what I'm doing."

The young Light priest smiled in return. "Thank you for your wisdom, my lady." He bowed before he headed back into the other suite.

I watched him as he re-entered. Shi Hua would definitely need her old friends to keep her sanity. I wished I could help her more, but her fate would be in the hands of the Twelve once I departed Jing.

That was the part of this mission I hated the most.

Chapter 26

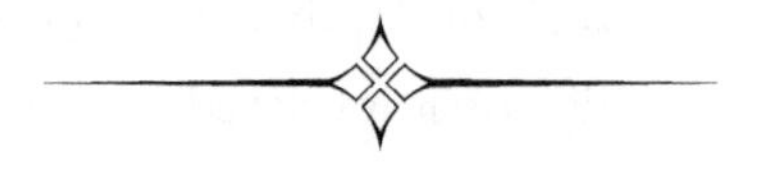

Shi Hua packed both hers and Yin Li's trunks shortly after dawn. She sat on the edge of the bed she'd shared with her aunt last night and waited.

Whatever Anthea had done when she left the suite and confronted Biming spurred Po to declare the imperial party would leave for Cheng-zhou the next morning. Except he hadn't come to bed with her. Yin Li claimed he felt she would provide more solace to Shi Hua. And while Shi Hua didn't believe her aunt lied, she felt guilty Po didn't think he would be allowed to or be able to comfort her. Or that she would deny him comfort.

Even more surprising was Anthea agreeing with Po about leaving Huang He. Shi Hua knew she wanted to participate in Justice Yi Nuo's interrogation of the captured female renegade. But whatever happened between her and Biming changed her mind, too.

At a knock on the bedchamber door, she called out, "Enter."

But it wasn't Mateqai or any of the other guards coming to collect the baggage for their journey to the capital. Po stepped inside and closed the door behind him.

"May we speak, Shi Hua?"

She smoothed her travel skirt, but she couldn't look at him. Couldn't deal with the disappointment in his eyes. Instead, she said, "I owe you an apology for my outburst last evening, Your Majesty. It was unbecoming as your wife, and it shall not happen again."

"Shi Hua, I beg you, please don't put more walls between us." He strode across the rug and sat beside her, but he didn't touch her. Instead, he rested his palms on his thighs. "My mother was unhappy for most of her life. As much as I loved my brother, his father made her miserable. I know ours is a political marriage, but I thought we were at least friends after all the years we've spent together. I don't want either of us to have the wretched life Mother did."

"Duty comes before happiness," she replied.

"Not even Chengwu believed that," he chided softly. "And while his was also a political marriage, he and his wife found ways to enjoy their lives together. And since you were involved in these conversations, you know he wasn't lying."

"But—" She shook. This was so much harder than she imagined.

"But what?" Po took her hand in his.

"I never thought Reverend Father Biming would view me as his way to control you." She looked up at Po. "I misjudged his reasons for encouraging me to accept your proposal."

The corners of his mouth lifted, and the gold beads decorating the ends of his moustache swayed. "I wouldn't worry about Biming. If Anthea's warning about how he treated you wasn't enough, Jin told Biming he would support her if she filed a complaint with our own Reverend Mother of Balance. And both Jian and Fa pointed out Biming foolishly tried to get the Issuran ambassador beheaded, which won't be taken with good grace by either Queen Teodora, the Issuran Reverend Mother of Balance, or their Reverend Father of Thief."

"But you—" Shi Hua stared at him. Had he really lied to his oldest, closest friend to protect her? She shook her head. "Surely he knows you were bluffing."

"Am I?" His smile widened into a grin. "We do have a contact scheduled with Teodora this morning. It will happen, just on the road instead of our suite."

"Are you sure you want to strike the hornet's nest?"

Po's grin faded. "I am supporting my empress. You addressed his behavior, and rather than correcting his attitude, he transgressed for a second time. I am going to report what happened to Teodora and the Issuran Reverend Father of Thief, and I'm going to ask their advice. Because if he is idiotic enough to cross you for a third time, I won't be able to stop Anthea from striking him with lightning. And we both know what she can do to a war ship."

She chuckled. "I wouldn't want her for an enemy."

"And I don't want you to ever think I won't watch your back, too. Yes, things will be hard, but I will do everything in my power to protect you." He leaned over and kissed her forehead.

At another knock on the bedchamber door, she reached out with her senses to discover a slightly impatient Mateqai.

"Enter," she called out.

He charged into the room and bowed. "Your Majesties, if you still want to leave within the next candlemark, we need to finish loading the wagons."

"The empress and her lady's trunks are ready, Captain." Po wore a slight smirk.

Stop, she said silently. *He's trying to do his job.*

Huizhong already had my trunk loaded, he teased.

She laughed at his double entendre. *The captain would not appreciate such a comment.*

Who's going to tell him? Po winked.

Mateqai leaned out the door. "Zhao, your assistance please." The guardsman and a couple of the duke's staff came in, lifted the trunks by their handles, and hauled them out of the bedchamber.

Po stood. "My lady, would you care to accompany me to my palace?"

She rose. "I would be delighted, my emperor."

Around First Afternoon, Shi Hua wished she was astride a horse instead of seated inside the stuffy carriage. Duke Lixin had provided the carriage for the royal couple, but only Yin Li rode inside with Shi Hua. Both Po and Yin Shang rode with the guards. The Huang He Temples provided mounts for the clergy and wardens accompanying them.

After such a bitter winter, Balance had responded with unusual heat, and it wasn't even technically spring yet. Both Shi Hua and Yin Li fanned themselves.

"I'd rather walk," Shi Hui grumbled.

"How long are you going to complain about the road you've chosen?" Yin Li folded her fan and eyed her.

"I wouldn't complain if it wasn't so hot in here." Shi Hua reached for the edge of the curtains.

Yin Li slapped Shi Hua's fingers with her fan.

"Ouch!" She rubbed her stinging skin. "What was that for?"

"You need to use your Twelve given common sense." Yin Li flipped open the fan and resumed waving it. "Po and Lixin had the imperial banners and emblems stripped from the carriage for a reason."

"And I've been dealing with assassins since I was ordained," Shi Hua shot back.

"You're their prime target, and now, we know why," Yin Li said coolly.

"What's that supposed to mean?"

"The renegades didn't want this marriage to happen."

Shi Hua stared at her aunt. "What makes you say that? There was no chance of that happening until they decided to murder the imperial family." When Yin Li said nothing, Shi Hua added, "You believe they have a seer?"

"How else could they have known the exact location of the *Mars Tranquilus* during our entire voyage?" Yin Li shrugged. "It also explains why Anthea has been targeted. You both keep upsetting their plans, and the bond you've forged makes you exponentially dangerous."

"Anthea falling through the demon portal wasn't an accident?" Shi Hua cocked her head,

Yin Li made a face at her. "Why else would Death and Balance step in to save her?"

Shi Hua leaned back against her seat and resumed fanning herself. There would be another attempt on one or both of them tonight. But she didn't need to be a seer to know that.

She just hoped the imperial entourage was up to the challenge.

Chapter 27

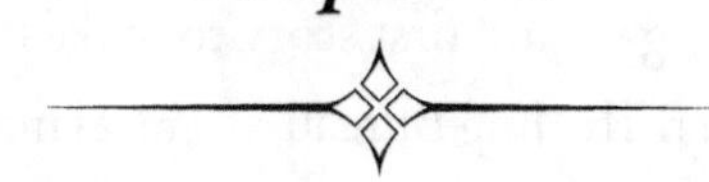

My buttocks and thighs ached when we reached the gate for the caravanserai where we would spend the night. It had been months since I rode for so many hours. The brick roads were well kept. However, traffic was rather light. Captain Huizhong mentioned merchants and entertainers wouldn't start their journeys until next First Day. A reminder that the Spring Rituals were a fortnight and three days away.

I'd always resented the Spring Rituals since Light and Balance were restricted on how we could participate. The edict last winter may have changed our privileges, but Luc had been trying to impregnate Sister Claudia of Love. Since I couldn't bear a child and Elizabeth had a special dispensation not to conceive after her torture at the hands of the skinwalkers, she and I spent the Spring Rituals drunk on blue agave wine when we weren't dealing with the queen's army and the refugees from Tandor along with semi-normal day-to-day court business.

My drinking during that time probably hadn't helped my stomach one bit.

The caravanserais of the eastern Old Continent were very different than the inns of the western North Long Continent. Out of tradition, most were hexagon-shaped, six sides for the Goddesses and six corners for the Gods. However, a caravanserai could have more or fewer exterior walls depending on location, building materials available, and the amount of traffic the caravanserai served.

The double-thick, two-story exterior served the same function as the walls around our cities. However, the individual rooms were built against the exterior walls. The first story held store fronts, warehouses, offices, and small one-room Temples. The second story consisted of the rooms of the inn itself.

The spacious open-air center courtyard housed the animals. It sloped down from the gate and first story to make loading and unloading pack animals easier. The Jing Bureau of Travel maintained a director and guards at every imperial caravanserai. They kept an account of everyone entering and leaving the facility.

When I asked why, Captain Huizhong said, "It's a holdover from the first demon invasion to ensure no one was taken by the enemy in the less populated areas of the empire. Now, it's mainly used to verify appropriate taxes are paid."

The accommodations couldn't compare with Duke Lixin's manse, but they were clean and comfortable. Local merchants were fascinated by Luc's steel crutches. The caravanserai's in-house blacksmith asked if she could make drawings of them. Her husband's knee had been crushed by an ill-tempered horse. Of course, Luc willingly agreed.

Our dinner was simple rice and mushrooms in broth, but it was quite tasty. The story Po gave to everyone claimed he was a merchant with a run of bad luck, losing his cargo in the fall of Tandor. Of course, that bit of news had traveled the world over last summer's trading season. It helped that several of us were eyewitnesses, and the tale kept the locals entertained.

Jonata tried not to laugh as she led me around the caravanserai like an ox. I kept my hood pulled low. My eyes were a sure identifier, and seeing my face clearly would destroy Po's carefully constructed semi-truth.

When we retired for the night, my buttocks and legs ached so miserably I couldn't sleep. Luc's soft snores made me want to suffocate him.

Yar and Jonata also slept soundly. Long Feather lay on a pallet across the doorway of our cell rather than sit outside our room. From the evenness of his breathing, he'd fallen asleep on guard duty. I'd chastise him in the morning. Since I was awake, I'd take the watch. I could always beg Shi Hua to let me ride in the carriage with her in the morning to sleep.

I stepped over Long Feather and reached for the thick curtain covering the doorway of our cell. He grabbed my left foot. I lost my balance and collapsed on top of him, dragging the curtain and its heavy rod with me.

His stubbornness and leverage were the only reasons the crossbow bolt missed me.

Chapter 28

"Assassin!"

The horrendous bellow woke Shi Hua from a sound sleep.

In time to see the shadow leaning over her.

Her heel shot at the shadow's knee while she flung one of Luc's flashbang Light spells at her assailant's face.

Her assailant screamed from his broken kneecap at the same time Yin Shang cried out. The figure in black collapsed over Shi Hua and Po's legs, a throwing knife in his back. Po yanked the head back and slit their assailant's throat for good measure.

Damn. Shi Hua really hated when she was right. But Anthea and the Reverend Fathers also posted guards outside of their rooms.

Anthea!

Stay away from the door! Someone's taking potshots at us with a crossbow!

Shi Hua rolled off her bed onto the floor. The slight gap between the wood planks and the heavy curtain allowed her to see how the assassin entered. Guardsman Zhao's unseeing eyes stared at her. His blood still oozed from the long cut across his neck.

He was one of the most competent men in Po's employ. That was the whole reason he'd come home to Jing with them. Queasiness filled her.

Everyone in the imperial party were the proverbial swimming ducks.

A crossbow bolt tore through the curtain above her head and buried its point into the opposing wall. That renegade with the crossbow would keep them pinned down. There was no other way out of the cell. If she couldn't come up with a plan, Po and the rest of her family were as dead as Zhao.

A high-pitched war cry in a language Shi Hua didn't recognize sounded across the open courtyard. More shouts and cries of pain followed.

She belly-crawled to her trunk stowed in the tiny space between the foot of her bed and the wall and opened it. After quickly stringing her bow, she counted her arrows.

Damn. There were only a half-dozen left. She should have bought more in Naha or Huang He. But no, she was too busy trying to play the good little empress. Enough was enough.

She closed her trunk, climbed on top of it, and yanked the curtain down. The two brackets snapped and the rod holding the curtain banged against the wood planks of the floor.

A crossbow bolt whistled through the air and plunged into the plaster of the opposing wall. Yin Li reached down and grabbed the end of the rod closest to her. The movement of the fabric as she slid the rod out of the curtain's hanging loops resulted in two more bolts that pinned the curtain to the floor.

"Shi Hua, do you know what you're doing?" Po whispered.

She glared at her husband, though he probably couldn't see her expression in the dark. "Yes, we need to get rid of that damn sniper," she hissed. "Now, shut up while we save your hide."

"Yes, my empress." She could hear his smirk in his words. And she was beginning to understand why other women found him so annoying at times.

She concentrated. *Anthea, can you freeze the demon spawn shooting at us?*

Which one? There's one on the roof and at least one, possibly more, on the second floor balcony across the courtyard.

Shi Hua bit her bottom lip. *Would it be easier to freeze the entire courtyard?*

Yes, but that will still leave the renegade on the roof and those of us in our rooms unaffected.

The sounds of hand-to-hand intensified below them. Innocent people were dying, and she needed to stop the violence.

That will work. Jian?

We're here, her old friend said silently. *We've lost one warden and Brother Muchen. Everyone else is pinned down.*

Shi Hua relayed her plan to Jian and Anthea.

Luc and I are ready, the justice reported.

As am I, Jian said.

Now! Shi Hua ordered as she squeezed her eyes shut.

Luc tossed a flashbang spell into the air above the courtyard. Confusion changed the tenor of the fighting in courtyard an instant before everything went silent.

Cursing came from the roof along with the sounds of two people hitting each other.

Shi Hua laid her own Light spell on her arrow, stepped into the doorway of their cell, and aimed at the first crossbowman. Jian did the same with the second, and they both released their projectiles. Of course, their arrows stopped the instant they entered Anthea's spell. She and Jian ducked back into their rooms.

Let go, Anthea, Shi Hua said.

The bedlam in the courtyard restarted. Shi Hua sensed her arrow strike its target, and her victim screamed, followed by a loud splash.

She peeked around the edge of the wall. The person she shot slumped against the balcony railing. Jian's target had somehow fallen into one of the watering troughs.

One of the figures fighting on the roof swept the legs of his opponent. The person fell backwards and started sliding down the tiles. They grabbed for a handhold, any handhold.

They snagged the edge of the last row of tiles and dangled in midair. But their weight was too much. The terracotta snapped and sent the person and an entire row of tiles plummeting into the courtyard. If they survive the initial fall, the heavy terracotta finished them off.

The surviving figure slipped through the roof frame that was no longer covered with tiles. Shi Hua whispered a quick prayer to Light it wasn't a renegade who survived and the occupants of the cell were safe.

She stepped into the doorway, knocked an arrow, and took aim at those fighting the caravanserai guards. Her remaining arrows were quickly used.

"Get back inside." Jian gestured sharply. His quiver was also empty. Fa prowled behind Jian. His white fur practically glowed in the dark.

The rest of the clergy and guardsmen poured out of their rooms now they were no longer pinned down. Shi Hua retreated into the room while Jian and Fa guarded them. The screaming and cursing and grunts from the courtyard gradually faded until only the moans of the injured and the weeping of the survivors remained.

Chapter 29

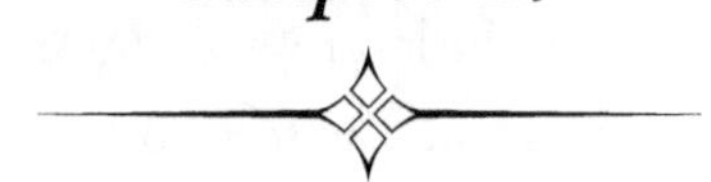

"I should have you lashed," I hissed at Long Feather as he followed me down the spiral staircase to the first story. My fury wasn't truly at him, but it didn't appear that any of the renegades survived to take my horrible mood out on.

"I'll remember that the next time a renegade starts shooting bolts at you, m'lady," he shot back.

I stopped short and glared at him. "I do not put up with that kind of behavior even from Little Bear."

"You have the right to reassign me when we return to Issura," he said fairly calmly. "Until then, my orders are to bring you home alive. No matter what it takes."

In the courtyard, the Light clergy and the caravanserai's resident Knowledge priest lit the area so we could see what we were dealing with. Unfortunately like Issura, Jing suffered from a lack of sufficient justices for every town, and the resupply depots between the major cities were essentially villages in and of themselves. Since the caravanserai was a day's ride from Huang He, the director said Chief Justice Li Chun would send a junior justice to them once every fortnight.

Of course, the next one wasn't due for another week.

Maybe it was a good thing none of the renegades lived. Dealing with them was too great a job for a circuit justice, much less a competent bureaucrat. Or any bureaucrat for that matter.

Which was probably why the caravanserai director was happy to accede his authority to Po and the Reverend Fathers.

As it was, the director had lost half his guards in the melee. The poor Death priestess looked positively overwhelmed at the number of corpses she had to deal with. She was used to the occasional death from injury or an older merchant passing in their sleep. Shi Hua commandeered some of the other travelers and took charge of dealing with the corpses.

My gut clenched. I'd forgotten she had to do the same thing after the Battle of Tandor. I would have helped too if Balance hadn't been trying to drown me and my brother Bumblebee.

The issue Luc and I faced were the group of mercenaries who'd fought against the renegades. They had surrendered to the wardens and imperial guardsmen with us, but they refused to remove their scarfs and hoods. The rough rasp of Conflict magic scraped along my nerves the closer we got to the group.

Do you feel that? I silently asked Luc.

Yes. He sounded as confused as I was. *What in Light is going on?*

The alleged mercenaries whispered among themselves at the sight of my eyes. In my rush, I'd forgotten to act blind as well as don my robes. So much for trying to keep my identity a secret. Jonata left her task of checking the renegade corpses for evidence and joined us as a precaution at the excited murmurs from the mercenaries we faced.

"Who does this belong to?" Yar roared. He stood by the pile of confiscated weapons, holding a sword in a leather scabbard.

None of the surrendered mercenaries said a thing. They weren't confused either.

Yar partially drew the weapon and examined it. A whisper of Thief magic emanated from the weapon. I crossed to the giant warden and touched the blade. Yes, definitely a Thief clergy weapon at one time.

I whirled and glared at the group. "Your aid tonight is most appreciated, but I cannot condone the possible theft of a Temple weapon. Explain your position to me so I might be able to grant you clemency."

"These are Skoloti markings," Yar added before he switched to a different language, one I didn't know.

Whatever he said must have convinced them. One of the taller mercenaries stepped forward and said in Jing, "It is mine."

"I am Chief Justice Anthea DiBalance of Orrin in Issura," I said.

The people surrounding her said something about the Red Justice. As much as I hated that nickname, I couldn't lose my temper here and now.

Custom dictated the woman answer me with her own name and rank. For a long moment, I didn't think she would speak.

Finally, she pushed back her hood and lowered her scarf. Yar gasped at the sight of her.

She lifted her chin. "Sister Darys DiThief of the Skoloti Tribes."

"I'm in Jing on a diplomatic mission," I said. "Why are you so far from home?"

"The assassination of Emperor Bao Chengwu prompted further investigation. I was sent to assess the situation, and if appropriate, offer aid to the crown prince when or if he returned to Jing." She smirked. "However, I aided instead of offering first. I hope you'll forgive me, Chief Justice."

I switched to Issuran and turned to Yar. "What is it about her you find unusual, Warden?"

"Her height and her white hair indicate she's descended from Themiscyreian seers."

"She doesn't appear to be elderly."

"She's not," Yar murmured. "Like a justice being born blind, the Themiscyreian seers are born with white hair."

I turned back to her and switched to Jing. "You do realize we will need to truthspell you and your people to verify your statement."

"I would expect no less from the justice tasked with bringing the Jing crown prince home."

"Can we please dispense with masks?" I gestured at Darys's followers.

She nodded. The people pushed back their hoods and lowered their scarves. Two of the women were tall like the thief priestess with the same melding of eastern and western Old Continent facial features. The rest had the general appearance of the eastern Old Continent, except the men all had scruffy beards.

"Shang?"

I turned to find Yin Li at the edge of the courtyard with Po and Yin Shang. Her hands covered her mouth. Her son's eyes were wide.

One of Darys's men stepped forward. "Yin Li?"

"Shang!" The Love priestess's scream was one of unadulterated joy. She raced across the courtyard and embraced the no-longer-missing Conflict priest. Little Yin Shang threw himself against his parents' legs.

Tears welled in my eyes. For once, someone I cared about had a happy ending.

Chapter 30

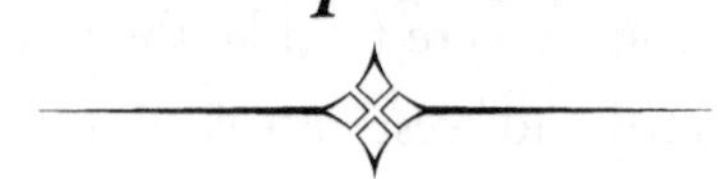

The woman shuffled to the cell at the end of the hall deep under a hill outside of the Jing capital of Chengzhou with a tray of bread, fruit, and plum wine. She wore peasant garb, and her knuckles were gnarled from hard work.

Four sentries stood guard in front of the cell door. One would say too many for a coddled, spoiled nobleman, but then Wu Sunshu was no ordinary noble.

Neither the woman nor the sentries spoke. In turn, each man inserted his key into a specific lock and twisted it. Once the door opened, she toddled inside, and the solid steel door slammed shut.

She dropped the illusion of age, sat the tray on the table the prisoner was permitted, and warded the room. "The first day's attempts all failed, Your Excellency."

Master Wu snorted, and his spell-threaded manacles jingled. "I swear Quan's spawn has more lives than a Kemet pharoah's cat."

She shrugged. "Eventually, his luck must run out. Also, he has already married the Light priestess."

"Your people were supposed to prevent that! You know what the seer foresaw!"

"She also warned you that trying to circumvent the future may cause the event you want to avoid to happen, Your Excellency." She cocked her head and waved to indicate the spacious cell. "Now may we free you from this indignity?"

"Not yet." Master Wu glared at the door. "Wait until that son of an irresponsible troublemaker arrives in Chengzhou. I want to see the light extinguished from his eyes as I crush his skull."

"As you wish, Your Excellency." She bowed and lowered her wards. After re-establishing her illusion, she knocked three times on the door. The guards let her out, and she was halfway up the corridor by the time the sentries finished locking the door.

The demons were right. The master had become a liability. It was time for her to take over what was left of the School of Sorcery and bring Jing back to its former glory.

Are Anthea and Luc ever going to get the royal couple to the capital of Jing to be crowned? Or will Wu Sunshu succeed in killing his stepson? Turn the page for a sneak peek at *A Cup of Conflict*!

A Cup of Conflict

I watched as Sister Yin Li of Love threw herself into the arms of her lost paramour, who we all thought was dead. Their young son followed suit. The reunited family laughed and cried and hugged.

He was quite a handsome man. I could understand why Yin Li was physically attracted to him. But the wave of emotion emanating from the pair was something far deeper. I leaned close to Luc and whispered, "So that's Shang."

I could feel my love turn to look at me. *Could you tone down the level of lust for another man you're sending my way?*

That isn't amusing.

I don't think so either. At least, you've now confirmed you were never physically attracted to Quan.

"That's what it took!" I glared at Luc.

Behind him, the Skoloti Sister of Thief Darys looked at us in confusion. Yar smirked. I had a feeling Jonata wore the same smirk behind me. Sister Yin Li of Love and High Brother Shang of Conflict were too busy kissing to pay any attention to the rest of us.

The merchants, who stopped here for the night on their way from the coast to the capital, drifted through the courtyard of the caravanserai and took inventory of their wares and stock that survived the battle. Shop keepers who resupplied travelers did the same. If it weren't for the forethought of Darys, Shang, and the rest of their rescue squad, everyone at this rest stop would be dead.

Crown Prince Bao Quan Po, heir to the Jing Empire, walked over and stood at my left side, but his attention was also on Yin Li and Shang. "She never kissed me like that."

"You were a worshipper, not her true love," I snapped.

"But still, with the size of my donations, I expect more," Po complained.

"I should be the only one receiving your donations, my husband." Bao Shi Hua, the soon to be empress consort of Jing, stalked through the mayhem, her bow still in her hand, and glared at her spouse.

A sly grin filled Po's face. "You never kiss me like that either."

The tiny woman reached up, grabbed the edges of his robe, and yanked him down for a thorough kiss. When she released him, she also smirked. A glance at his silk pants said why. "What were you saying?"

"Not a blessed thing, my wife." He released a deep breath. "Should we rent a cell for Yin Li and Shang so we may have some privacy?"

"I'll take care of it." I made a shooing motion. "Please go back to your room before you feel the need for another public display of affection."

The royal couple held hands as they retreated to the spiral stone staircase leading to the second story. It was good to see them showing some affection. While Shi Hua was only interested in women and Po was interested in anything that moved, I was glad they were trying to make their political marriage work.

"Should we interrupt?" I asked Luc.

"Quan and Shi Hua or Shang and Yin Li?"

I eyed my own paramour. "If you interrupt the prince, he will ask you to join them."

"Unfortunate, but true." Luc shot me a wicked grin. "Maybe if we both join them?"

I held up my hand. "You are on your own for this one, High Broth-er. I'm going to take a soma tear and try to get some sleep." I turned to head up the same stairs the prince and his wife had just climbed.

"Wait, Chief Justice," Sister Darys called out. "Aren't you going to question me and my party? We could be renegades for all you know."

I pivoted to face her. "Sister, I already know you aren't a skinwalker. If you're a demon, you would have ripped out both my throat and the Lady Shi Hua's a few moments ago when we were standing next to each other. And if you're a renegade, all I ask is that you let me have a good night's sleep and a cup of Jing black tea in the morning before you poi-son me. Again."

I walked toward the staircase once again. Frankly, Reverend Father Jin and Reverend Father Biming were responsible for truthspelling the newcomers in order to protect their soon-to-be crowned emperor. And Balance help me, I was mightily tired of doing their job.

"Excuse me!" Shi Hua's shout actually broke Yin Li and Shang's embrace.

I looked up to find the empress-to-be leaning over the balcony rail-ing. Everyone in the courtyard quieted.

"Can someone please remove the dead assassin in our bed? The crown prince and I are trying to conceive an heir!"

◆

Acknowledgments

As most of my readers know, 2022 was a very rough year for me personally. Too many losses wears on a person.

However, I've been lucky enough to have writing friends who've kept my spirits up and tried to keep me on track. To Angie, Candi, Julie, Kate, and Tracie, a heartfelt thank you!

To Becky, thank you for allowing me to hide in your spare bedroom for a weekend and just have some girl talk time.

Apparently, the universe knew I would need extra support, and it reconnected me with Amanda, Gretchen, and Kathy, long ago friends who I'm glad are back in my life.

To Elaina and Jaye, you've become more than my cover artist and my formatter, and I'm glad I've gotten to know you both.

And finally, to Darling Husband, Genius Kid, Princess Bella, and the Grandpuppy, you remind me that family is the core of a good life.

WORDS AND PHRASES SPECIFIC TO THE JUSTICE SERIES

Anacapa Islands – a series of four islands off the southwestern coast of Issura. Limuw is the largest. Wi'ma is the second largest. Anacapa is the closest to Orrin. Tuqan is the furthest from Orrin.

Apprentice – lowest rank of a trade or craft guild

Berda – gender fluid; someone who does not stick to traditional gender roles

Britannia – Toscan name for a series of islands off the western coast of the Old Continent. The two largest are Eire and Albion. Four hundred years before Anthea's time, the queens of Eire and Albion were losing their battle against the demons. They ordered the islands evacuated and the Temples of Death to launch their last resort spells. The islands are now barren, and no one who steps on them lives for long.

Briton Diaspora – refers to the survivors and their descendants of the evacuation of Britannia who are now scattered around the world

Brother – title for any fully ordained priest of any Temple that accepts men, except for the Temple of Father

Cant – Issura's neighboring nation-state to the south

Chengzhou – the capital of Jing, a nation-state on the eastern shore of the Old Continent

Chief Justice – title of the highest ranked priestess at a Temple of Balance

Chief [name of trade] – the highest ranking master guild member of a trade in a city or region

The Cradle – according to legend, the continent where Child created the first members of the human race

Duke/Duchess – highest ranking noble of a region

Distance-view glasses – a telescope

Father – title for any fully ordained priest of the Temple of Father

Gilwas – a city in northern Issura

Gray Mountains – a mountain range that runs the entire length of the western side of the Long Continents

The Grand Canal – a human-built canal that passes through the isthmus connecting the Long Continents

The Great Forest – the rainforest that covers nearly half of the Southern Long Continent on its north side

The Green Lady Inn – an inn near the Embassy District of Orrin, it had the only entrance/exit to the tunnel system within the city walls that was not a Temple until it was bricked over and magically sealed after the events of *A Modicum of Truth* and *A Matter of Death*.

Guild – a civil organization for a trade or craft

Guild Master – an expert tradesman's rank based on analysis of his/her peers

Healer – a person with the magical ability to heal illness and repair wounds

High Brother – title of the chief priest of a city Temple, except the Temple of Father

High Father – title of the chief priest of a city's Temple of Father

High Mother – title of the chief priestess of a city's Temple of Mother

High Sister – title of the chief priestess of a city Temple, except the Temples of Balance and Mother

Iberia – nation-state on the southwestern corner of the Old Continent

Issura – queendom on the western coast of Northern Long Continent; the Peaceful Sea forms its western border with the nation of Pagonia to the north, the nation of Cant to the south, the nations of the Cliffdwellers and Diné to the southeast and the Gray Mountains to the east

Jing – nation-state on the eastern side of the Old Continent

Journeyman/Journeywoman – middle rank of a trade or craft guild

Justice – title for any fully ordained priestess of the Temple of Balance; alternate term of address is Lady Justice

Kemet – nation-state on the northeast corner of the Cradle

Kulshra'jek Pass – a pass through the Gray Mountains adjacent to Pana Valley, mainly used by Comanche traders in the summer on their way west

Lake Tulamniu – a lake at the south end of Pana Valley

The Levant – a loose alliance of Phoenician city-states between the Hittite Empire and Kemet on the eastern side of the Middle Sea

The Long Continents – the two continents separating the Peaceful Sea from the Panthalassa Sea, they are connected by a narrow isthmus

The Lost Continent – the southern continent between the Peaceful Sea and the Storm Sea. By Anthea's time, the original inhabitants were believed to be slaughtered by demons 500 years before. Sailors from the Sea Peoples and Maurya who landed there after the inhabitants' disappearance reported screams but found no one. Those with magic talents went mad. Not even the priests and priestesses from Child could save them. Those who tried went mad themselves.

Magistrate – elected official of a city or town in Issura who is responsible for civil and criminal law enforcement and the city or town's defense/care in an emergency

Master – senior member of a trade or craft guild; or the clergyperson who is primarily responsible for the training of a novice class

Maurya – the southern-most nation of the Old Continent

Middle Sea – the shallow sea that separates The Cradle from the Old Continent

Mother – title for any fully ordained priestess of the Temple of Mother

Naha – capital of the Kingdom of Ryukyu, a set of islands in the Peaceful Sea southwest of the Fire Islands

National Road – main, paved road through the nation of Issura. It roughly parallels the western coastline.

New Thenos – an island city/state on the eastern coast of the Northern Long Continent

Novice – a person in training to become a priest/priestess of the Twelve

Orrin – third largest city in the queendom of Issura with the second largest port

Pagonia – Issura's neighboring nation to the north

Panthalassa Sea – the ocean that separates the Long Continents from the western part of the Old Continent and the Cradle

Peaceful Sea – the ocean that separates the Long Continents from the eastern part of the Old Continent, the islands and archipelagos of the Sea Peoples, and the Lost Continent

Peacekeepers – men and women who act as an Issuran city's police force. They report to the city's magistrate. They also act as an auxiliary defense force if their city or nation is attacked.

Pimu – one of a series of four islands off the northern coast of Cant

Rambla – formerly the northernmost city in Cant, its people were used to hatch demon eggs during the events of *A Modicum of Truth*

Redwood Grove – a fair-sized town in the northeastern section of the Duchy of Orrin. It nestles on a plateau in the foothills of the Grey Mountains near the border with the Duchy of Pana.

Reverend Father – senior-most priest of a Temple order, the leader of that sect in the nation in which he resides

Reverend Mother – senior-most priestess of a Temple order, the leader of that sect in the nation in which she resides

Ryukyu – a kingdom consisting of a set of islands in the Peaceful Sea southwest of the Fire Islands

Seat – person holding the highest ranking position of a Temple

Shakya – nation-state in the western portion of the Old Continent, southwest of Jing and northeast of Maurya

Sister – title for any fully ordained priestess of any Temple that accepts women, except for the Temples of Mother and Balance

Skinwalker – a human with talent who performs demon magic; the magic corrupts their physical body to the point they need another person's skin to contain their spirit

Standora – capital and largest city of Issura

Storm Sea – ocean bordered by the eastern part of the Cradle, the southern part of the Old Continent, and the western part of the Lost Continent

Tandor – Issuran city that guards the border with Cant and Diné

Temple – a collection of people dedicated to the service of one of the twelve gods; a building that houses such people; the primary place of worship for one of the twelve gods

Tiwan – the capital of Cant

Toscana – nation-state on the southern section of the Old Continent; location of the first battle against the demons

Tupi – one of the indigenous tribes of the Great Forest, they are known for their Vintner's variety of medicinal plants

The Twelve – the collective name for the twelve deities of the Justice universe

The United Dulohans – a series of islands south of the islands that make up the Kingdom of Ryukyu

Valencia – duchy in the nation-state of Iberia; know for their innovative shipbuilding designs

Valley of the Lost – the desert between Issura, Diné, and the Cliffdweller Territory

Warden – security guard of a Temple, they act as supplementary military personnel in the event of a demon invasion

Wechuge – a human who commits the sin of cannibalism, they are transformed into a creature of ice and magic

Xiongnu Confederation – a collection of nomadic tribes north of Jing

THE TWELVE TEMPLES

MOTHER

Cloak Color – Light blue

Motto – "To give without thought; to forgive with love."

The Temple of Mother is responsible for the teaching of household arts, such as spinning, weaving, food storage and preparation. The order is also responsible for caring for those who have lost their families.

FATHER

Cloak Color – Dark blue

Motto – "All tools are weapons, and weapons tools."

The Temple of Father is responsible for the constructive arts, such as carpentry and smithing.

Balance

Cloak Color – Black

Motto – "Balance in all things."

The Temple of Balance runs the judicial system. A justice is the judge in criminal and civil cases.

Light

Cloak Color – Medium brown

Motto – "Light brings truth, for without truth, there can be no justice."

The Temple of Light is responsible for codifying contracts and mediating contract disputes. A Light priest also acts as the bailiff for a justice, and is often the one to truthspell a witness or the accused. The Temple of Light also provides military support to a nation's civilian army.

Knowledge

Cloak Color – Gold

Motto – "With patience, knowledge comes."

The Temple of Knowledge is responsible for education and for recording historical events. They essentially act as the library system for the Justice universe.

Thief

Cloak Color – Grey

Motto – "Hiding in plain sight."

The Temple of Thief acts as the intelligence-gathering arm of both the Temples and the civilian leaders. They finance their efforts through gambling dens.

Conflict

Cloak Color – Dark Red

Motto – "Destruction is the necessary evil, for it clears the way for new growth."

The Temple of Conflict focuses on strategy and all martial arts. They are the primary support and teachers of a nation's army.

Love

Cloak Color – Medium Red

Motto – "Pleasure is life."

The Temple of Love are the holy prostitutes. They also deal with sex education and lead the Spring Rituals, the annual fertility rites which were first used to breed as many humans with magical talent as possible. Don't underestimate them. They fight just as hard and as nasty as their fellow clergy in Conflict.

Child

Cloak Color – Light green

Motto – "All things are new once."

The Temple of Child is responsible for the emotional health of citizens. They also develop and teach agriculture and animal husbandry techniques.

WILDING

Cloak Color – Dark green

Motto – "All creatures return to us."

The Temple of the Wildling God deals with management of wild animal populations, forestry, and the protection of ecosystems.

VINTNER

Cloak Color – Purple

Motto – "The line between wisdom and madness is one sip."

The Temple of Vintner not only deals with the cultivation of grapes and the production of wine, but they also promote the gathering, cultivation and processing of all medicinal herbs.

DEATH

Cloak Color – Black

Motto – "For every life, there is a death."

The Temple of Death takes care of the gathering of the dead, the last rites, and disposal of the corpses. They also act as a repository for the last wills and testaments of all citizens.

CHARACTERS AND PLACES

QUEENDOM OF ISURRA

ORRIN

TEMPLE OF BALANCE

Chief Justice Anthea – a circuit justice for ten winters until her appointment as Chief Justice of Orrin at the age of thirty winters ("Justice")

Chief Justice Penelope – deceased, predecessor to Anthea as Chief Justice of Orrin

Chief Justice Thalia – deceased, predecessor to Penelope as Chief Justice of Orrin, maternal grandmother of Anthea

Justice Yanaba – junior justice assigned to the city of Orrin after the events of *A Question of Balance*

Justice Erato – junior justice assigned to the circuit of the eastern section of the duchy of Orrin and the southern tip of the duchy of Pana Valley after Anthea is sentenced to the seat of Orrin in "Justice"

Sivan – personal assistant to Chief Justice Anthea and head of the household staff

Donella – senior clerk

Lailani – junior clerk

Chief Warden Little Bear – head of the Balance wardens

Warden Tyra – junior warden, killed in the Battle of Tandor (*A Matter of Death*)

Warden Gina – junior warden, promoted to chief warden of Balance under Chief Justice Elizabeth when she is reassigned to the new Duchy of Anacapa

Warden Aglaia – junior warden, died in the battle to retake the Temple of Love (*A Question of Balance*)

Warden Daniel – junior warden, non-talented

Warden Noko – junior warden

Warden Jonata – junior warden, Aglaia's replacement from the Standora Wardens' Academy, a passive talent

Warden Dezba – junior warden

Warden Tahoma – junior warden

Warden Ahiga – junior warden, non-talented

Warden Long Feather – junior warden

Warden Ailyn – junior warden, she replaced Tyra after her death

Warden Mylon – junior warden, died during the events of *A Hand of Father*

Hogarth – former chief warden under Justices Thalia and Penelope, now stablemaster, husband of Deborah

Deborah – Head cook, wife of Hogarth

Nathan – squire to Chief Justice Anthea after he was sentenced to pay reparations for stealing bread, an orphan, age ten winters at the time of his sentencing in *A Question of Balance*

Ming Wei – squire to Justice Yanaba, nine winters old at the end of *A Question of Balance*. Originally from Jing, she was sold by her parents to a Jing noble as a sex slave and brought to Issura. When the noble's crimes were discovered, he immolated himself and his slaves. Ming Wei was the only survivor and has severe scar tissue on her face, back and arms.

Kosumi – the son of Justice Yanaba and High Brother Xander, conceived due to the breeding edict issued worldwide by the Reverend Mothers of Justice and the Reverend Fathers of Light, born between the events of *A Hand of Father* and *A Measure of Knowledge*

Temple of Light

High Brother Luc – a circuit priest for twelve winters until his appointment as the seat at the age of thirty-two winters between the events of "Justice" and "Diplomacy in the Dark"

High Brother Kam – semi-retired, predecessor to Luc as chief priest, poisoned and died during the events of *A Question of Balance*

Brother Mat – Second to Luc. His birth name is Micah. He murdered the real

Mat on his way to Orrin from Standora. Died under Anthea's truthspell interrogation in *A Question of Balance*.

Brother Jeremy – youngest junior priest until he is promoted to Luc's second after the events of *A Question of Balance*.

Brother Garbhan – junior priest who is assigned permanently to Orrin after the events of *A Matter of Death*

Brother Wolf Run – junior priest partnered with Justice Erato on the eastern Orrin circuit

Istaqa – personal assistant to High Brother Luc and head of the household staff

Edberth – former personal assistant to High Brother Kam, he now acts as evening assistant to High Brother Luc

Henry – stablemaster

Chief Warden Nicholas – head of the Light wardens

Warden Gibb – junior warden, died shortly after the renegades' kidnapping of High Brother Luc in *A Question of Balance*

Warden Mateqai – junior warden, becomes Sister Shi Hua's personal bodyguard during the events of *A Modicum of Truth*

Warden Yar – junior warden

Warden Tadhg – junior warden

Warden Gad – junior warden

Chao – the son of Sister Shi Hua and Brother Jeremy, conceived due to the breeding edict issued worldwide by the Reverend Mothers of Justice and the Reverend Fathers of Light, born between the events of *A Hand of Father* and *A Measure of Knowledge*

Temple of Love

High Sister Gerd – chief priestess, biological daughter of Thalia and Kam, biological mother of Anthea. She was removed from office on charges of fraud, bribery of a public official, unlawful magic, and conspiracy to commit murder. Later, the charges of dealing in demon artifacts and treason were added. Beheaded by Anthea during the event of *A Twist of Love*.

Sister Dragonfly – Gerd's second, *berda* (genderfluid), is acting High Sister after the events in *A Question of Balance*, becomes High Sister after the events in *A Modicum of Truth*

Sister Gretchen – junior priestess, deceased. The discovery of her body in one of Duke Marco's wine barrels precipitates the events in *A Question of Balance*.

Sister Claudia – junior priestess, Dragonfly's second, some Light talent

Sister Shada – junior priestess

Sister Zihna – junior priestess

Sister Ilina – Gerd's second until her death; Lady Katarina DiMara's biological mother; she died of the wasting disease a year prior to "Justice"

Chief Warden Citana – new chief warden of Love after renegades killed and replaced the entire warden contingent of the Temple

Warden Jocasta – junior warden, one of the replacement wardens after the events of *A Question of Balance*

Warden Ekta – junior warden

Gregorios – a eunuch who was High Sister Dragonfly's personal assistant and head of household until their murder prior to the beginning of *A Twist of Love*

Ichik – a eunuch who is Sister Claudia's personal assistant

Iona – Love's maintenance person, she does minor repairs and servicing of the Temple

Temple of Conflict

High Brother Han – chief priest

Brother Piru – junior priest, Han's second

Sister Migina – junior priestess

Brother Yas – junior priest

Brother Keanu – junior priest

Temple of Death

High Sister Bertrice – chief priestess

High Brother Kai – deceased, predecessor of Bertrice, retired in Bertrice's favor as the temple seat and became a teaching brother in Standora until his death

Brother Xander – Bertrice's second until her demise during the Battle of Tandor, succeeds her as Orrin's High Brother of Death

Sister Raven Claw – Xander's second when he becomes high brother

Brother Elu – junior priest

Chief Warden Axton – head of the Death wardens

Warden Hitari – junior warden

Temple of Vintner

High Brother Ben – chief priest

Sister Nina – junior priestess

Chief Warden Mangas – head of the Vintner wardens

Warden Golden Eagle – junior warden, murdered by Gerd during the events of *A Twist of Love*

TEMPLE OF MOTHER

High Mother Bianca – chief priestess, she commits suicide when Anthea discovers Bianca has been selling children

High Mother Leocadia – chief priestess, she transferred from the Temple in Gilwas and succeeded Bianca between the events in *A Touch of Mother* and *A Twist of Love*

Mother Kalama – junior priestess with Light talent

Chief Warden Maebh – head of the Mother wardens until the events of *A Touch of Mother*

Ademaro – Leocadia's personal chef she brought with her from Gilwas

TEMPLE OF FATHER

High Father Jerrod – chief priest

TEMPLE OF CHILD

High Sister Mya – chief priestess

Brother Turtle – junior priest, helps to save Justice Yanaba by pulling her soul back into her body during the events of *A Modicum of Truth*

Sister Dawn Star – junior priestess

Makawee – Child's head of household and Mya's personal assistant

Chief Warden High Rock – head of the Child wardens

Temple of Wildling

High Brother Jax – chief priest, second form is a wolf

Sister Farrah – Jax's second, second form is a fox

TEMPLE OF THIEF

High Brother Talbert – chief priest

Sister Cedar Grove – Talbert's second

Brother Teluhci – junior priest

Sister Malila – junior priestess

Chief Warden Sabine – head of the Thief wardens

TEMPLE OF KNOWLEDGE

High Sister Mariana – chief priestess

Brother Luca – junior priest

NOBILITY

Duke Benedetto DiMara – father of Marco, Alessa, and Isabella, husband of Cora, convicted of conspiracy to use illegal magic to mind wipe his son Marco during the events of "Justice"; imprisoned at Standora for life.

Lady Cora DiMara – mother of Marco, Alessa, and Isabella, convicted of treason and demon dealing, executed by the Reverend Mother Alara of Balance during the events of "Justice".

Duke Marco DiMara – duke of Orrin, inherited his post at the age of eighteen winters after his parents were found guilty of numerous offenses and stripped of their titles and property

Lady Katarina DiMara (nee' DiLove) – common-born wife of Marco, animal healer. Her mother was Sister Ilina, a priestess of the Temple of Love who died of the wasting sickness the summer before Katarina's eighteenth winter.

Lord Kam DiMara – eldest child of Marco and Katarina and heir to the Duchy of Orrin, named for High Brother Kam of Light, godson of Chief Justice Anthea and High Brother Luc

Lady Alessa DiMara – sister of Marco, a passive talent, lover of Sister Gretchen of Love

Lady Isabella DiMara – sister of Marco, attends the University of Standora

Bartholomew – retainer of Duke Marco's until it was learned he'd assaulted Lady Alessa and Sister Gretchen. Lady Alessa subsequently asked Chief Justice Anthea for clemency and hired him to manage the estates Sister Gretchen had bequeathed to Alessa.

William – retainer of Duke Marco's

Julian – retainer of Duke Marco's

Noemi – a handmaid to Lady Alessa

Arturo – former captain of Duke Marco's flagship. His murder is the precipitating event of "Diplomacy in the Dark".

Titus – captain of Duke Marco's flagship, the *Mars Tranquilus*

Lady Aurora – a noblewoman who commissioned a ceremonial silver knife as a gift to her groom from Govind, Anthea confiscated the knife in order to kill a wechuge

CITIZENS

Malven DiCook – duly elected magistrate of Orrin

Dante – one of Orrin's peacekeepers, dies at the beginning of *A Modicum of Truth*

Barbora – wife of Dante, dies at the beginning of *A Modicum of Truth*

Jaime – one of Orrin's peacekeepers

Leyti – one of Orrin's peacekeepers

Fat Squirrel – one of Orrin's peacekeepers

Drest – a peacekeeper, dismissed by DiCook for extortion

Robin – a peacekeeper, dismissed by DiCook for warning Drest that DiCook was coming to arrest him

Alo – an innkeeper, the owner of the Green Lady Inn near the Embassy District

Xoco – Alo's wife who died giving birth to Chumana

Chumana – Alo's daughter, she is ten winters at the beginning of *A Question of Balance*

Cat and Dog – the leaders of Orrin's street children, Chief Justice Anthea uses them to obtain information outside of the normal Temple intelligence channels

Harold – an Orrin wagoneer

GUILDS

Chief Healer Aaron – head of the Healers' Guild

Master Healer Devin – second to Aaron in the Orrin Healer's Guild, originally from New Thenos

Journeywoman Bly – a junior healer, often assists Master Devin at autopsies, later a master healer in her own right

Simi – Bly's apprentice at the Healers Guild when Bly attains master status

Master Healer Una – a master healer who specializes in head trauma and sleep disorders, she also happens to be a dreamwalker

EAGLE REACH

Kele – a farmer outside of the village, Hania's brother

Pavati – Kele's daughter who went missing on her way to Redwood Grove before the events of *A Virtue of Child*

REDWOOD GROVE

Hania – a farmer outside of the town, Kele's brother

TANDOR

High Brother Dav – chief priest of the Temple of Light, dies during the events of *A Modicum of Truth*

Chief Justice Elizabeth – chief justice of the Temple of Balance, later becomes chief justice of the Duchy of Anacapa

Minerva – the new clerk with the Temple of Balance, a renegade, killed during the fight within the Temple of Balance (*A Modicum of Truth*)

High Brother Aduba – chief priest of the Temple of Conflict

Brother Tighan – second of the Temple of Conflict, a renegade, killed by Aduba during the fall of Tandor

High Brother Nantan – chief priest of the Temple of Death

Sister Reby – second of the Temple of the Wildling God, first introduced as a shapeshifting thief in "The Perfect Partner", second form is a polecat

Brother Sisquoc – priest of the Temple of the Wildling God, second form is a panther. He's transferred to the Orrin Temple of the Wildling God after the events of *A Matter of Death*.

Brother Trajan – priest of the Temple of the Wilding God, second form is a wolf

Sister Jumping Mouse – priestess of the Temple of the Wildling God, second form is a kangaroo rat

Duke Enzo DiToscana – Duke of Tandor, murdered by a skinwalker possessing his wife

Duchess Nadine DiToscana – the widow of Duke Enzo of Tandor, becomes the Duchess of Anacapa in her own right after the events of *A Matter of Death*

Ural DiSand – merchant from Tandor, implicated in the Assassin Guild plots in Orrin, killed while possessed by a skinwalker during *A Modicum of Truth*

Amarantha DiRoma – Tandoran merchant, rival of Ural DiSand, murdered by renegades shortly before they poisoned most of the personnel of the Tandoran Temples

Govind – a silversmith who assisted with the defense of Tandor against the demon army, settled in Orrin after the evacuation and fall of Tandor

The Wave Dancer – Duchess Nadine of Tandor's flagship, one of two remaining ships in Tandor prior to the Battle of Tandor

STANDORA – CAPITAL CITY OF ISSURA

Reverend Mother Alara – head of Issura's Temple of Balance

Justice Rose – novice training priestess of the main Temple of Balance in Standora when Anthea was a novice

Justice Melanippe – a novice in Anthea's class. She was the top student, but she was also recruited by Thief to report on any wrongdoing in Balance. She disappeared from the home Temple of Balance in Standora between the events of *A Virtue of Child* and *A Hand of Father*.

Reverend Father Farrell – head of Issura's Temple of Light

Brother Elroy – a Light priest, aide to Reverend Father Farrell, and a distance speaker who accompanies the Isurran and Sea Peoples fleets to Tandor in *A Matter of Death*

Brother Long Wind – a Light priest and aide to Reverend Father Farrell; he accompanies the queen's army to Tandor in *A Matter of Death*

Brother Garbhan – a Light priest and aide to Reverend Father Farrell; he remains in Orrin during and after the events of *A Matter of Death*

Brother Jon – novice training priest at the main Temple of Light in Standora, murdered by the skinwalker at Samael DiRoy's abandoned manse prior to *A Question of Balance*

Brother Gáagii – a junior Light priest

Reverend Mother Sxa'min – head of Issura's Temple of Love

High Sister Imala – a Love priestess, considered to be the lead contender for position of Reverend Mother of Love; she accompanies the queen's army in *A Matter of Death*

Chief Warden Catherine – Imala's chief warden; she was a classmate of Mateqai's at the Warden Academy and the two had a physical relationship

Warden Hototo – a junior Love warden

Reverend Father Grey Shadow – head of Issura's Temple of Thief

Brother White Wolf – a senior priest of Thief; he's a personal friend of High Sister Imala

Queen Teodora – reigning monarch of Issura

Crown Princess Chiara – eldest child and heir of Queen Teodora of Issura; lady general of the queen's army

Duke White Eagle – former Conflict brother, left the order to marry Crown Princess Chiara; honorary title Duke of Standora as the future queen's consort; lord general of the queen's army

PANA VALLEY

Lord Aleister DeGrove – noble noted for his vineyards

JING EMPIRE

CHENGZHOU

Empress Bao De – ruler of Jing a century before Bao Yu, she sacrificed herself and her consort to stop a demon army

Empress Bao Yu – ruler of Jing until her death from natural causes during "Courting Trouble"

Emperor Bao Chengwu – ruler of Jing until his assassination by demons, succeeded his mother Bao Yu during "Courting Trouble"

Crown Prince Bao Quan Po, formerly Ambassador Quan Po – half-brother of Emperor Bao Chengwu; son of Empress Bao Yu and Quan; was heir to the throne until his eldest nephew was born; became heir to the Dragon Throne with the assassinations of his brother and nephews

Wu Sunshu – imperial consort of Empress Bao Yu, master of the School of Sorcery, imprisoned for life on the charge of treason

Reverend Father Jin – head of Jing's Temple of Light

Sister Shi Hua – a priestess of Light, who was tapped as Po's bodyguard. She received additional training from Conflict, Thief, and Love. Originally from the town of Yintze in the southern province of Chu.

Brother Lin – novice master of Light

Brother Jian – a priest of Light, classmate of Shi Hua during their novice years

Brother Fa – a Wildling priest, his second form is a tiger, a friend of Shi Hua and Jian during their novice years

Justice Mei Wen – a priestess of Balance, Shi Hua's closest friend other than Jian during their novice years

Sister Yin Li – a priestess of Love, Shi Hua's maternal aunt

Yin Shang – the son of Sister Yin Li and Brother Shang, he's five winters when he first appeared in *A Touch of Mother*

Reverend Father Chen – head of Jing's Temple of Conflict

Reverend Father Feng – replaced Chen after the disappearance of him and his army before *A Touch of Mother*

Brother Shang – a priest of Conflict, Shi Hua's instructor when she was a novice; lover of Yin Li and father of Yin Shang; last seen with Reverend Father Chen's army

Reverend Father Biming – head of Jing's Temple of Thief

Duke Zixin – a third cousin of Quan Po who believes he has a superior claim to the Jing throne due to his noble birth

The Unbridled – a spy ship used by the Temple of Thief, a four-masted carrack built in the Iberian duchy of Valencia, captained by Reverend Father Biming during *A Modicum of Truth*

Brother Hadar – a priest of Thief from the Kingdom of Hejaz, serving on board *The Unbridled*

ISLANDS OF THE SEA PEOPLES

KINGDOM OF O'AHU

Prince Alika – youngest son of the king of the Sea Peoples, one of Sister Gretchen's worshippers, the father of her unborn child

Captain Iakepa – senior captain of the O'ahu trading fleet

DINÉ NATION

AJÉÍ (HEART)

Temple of Balance

Reverend Mother Hózhó – head of the Diné Temple of Balance

Justice Mosi – a junior justice

Justice Spotted Fawn – the western circuit justice for the Diné Nation, killed in the Battle of Tandor

Bidzii – Spotted Fawn's clerk, he was fluent in Issuran so the justice spoke through him; killed in the Battle of Tandor

TEMPLE OF LIGHT

Brother Bumblebee – junior priest of Light with the Diné army, Anthea's half-brother by her father Kilchii

TEMPLE OF CONFLICT

Reverend Father Kilchii – head of the Diné Temple of Conflict. When he first met Anthea, he gave his name as "Nizhé'é", which in the Diné language means "your father" because he is her biological father.

TEMPLE OF KNOWLEDGE

Sister Lizard – junior priestess with the Diné army at Tandor

TEMPLE OF THIEF

Sister Shideezhi – junior priestess, Anthea's half-sister by their father Kilchii

TEMPLE OF WILDLING

Sister Cheona – junior priestess, her second form is a panther

ELDERS

Matriarch Nascha – elected leader of the Diné Nation, a clan elder

Elder Johona – a clan elder

Elder Chooli – a clan elder who was murdered to fuel the hatching of a demon egg during the events of *A Hand of Father*

CITIZENS

Niyol – Nacha's eldest brother

Sike – Johona's eldest brother, a suitor of Matriarch Nascha, he was murdered during *A Hand of Father*

Tibah – deceased, Chief Justice Thalia's mother, Reverend Mother Hózhó and Matriarch Nascha's great-aunt, and Chief Justice Anthea's great-grandmother

CLIFFDWELLERS

Healer Kotori – a physician with the Diné army during the siege of Tandor

PLAINS NATIONS – COMANCHE

High Brother Pecos – a senior Conflict priest with the Diné army during the siege of Tandor, Anthea's half-brother through their father Kilchii

THE KINGDOM OF RYUKYU

NAHA

Temple of Thief

Reverend Father Ogusuku – head of the Ryukyu Temple of Thief

Sister Jade – junior priestess, assigned as Anthea and Shi Hua's bodyguard while they were in Ryukyu

Sister Jasmine – junior priestess, assigned as Anthea and Shi Hua's bodyguard while they were in Ryukyu